Born in Moose Jaw, Saskatchewan, Canada, Wesley grew up in the small town of Marshall, Saskatchewan. After graduating from the University of Regina in 2013 with a degree in History, he worked in the entertainment industry for four years before penning his first work, *Dreams*. He currently resides in Regina, Saskatchewan.

For my family.

Wesley McBride

Dreams

AUSTIN MACAULEY PUBLISHERS™
LONDON • CAMBRIDGE • NEW YORK • SHARJAH

A CIP catalogue record for this title is available from the British Library.

ISBN 9781788786959 (Paperback)
ISBN 9781788786966 (Hardback)
ISBN 9781528955911 (ePub e-book)

www.austinmacauley.com

First Published (2019)
Austin Macauley Publishers Ltd
25 Canada Square
Canary Wharf
London
E14 5LQ

He was dizzy and breathing heavily. He stood, gripping the railing bolted to the eroded concrete in front of the door. His hand tremored as he weakly gripped the handle and fell inside. A crack. It was dark. On his knees now. Slowly moving forward. Something hard against my head. His eyes were closed now but he kept a hand on the wall that was guiding him. It was the longest wall. So long. Too many turns. Now gone. He felt softness on his face, though he could no longer describe that sensation. A camera still rolling but no film.

It was a Friday. Faint noises of traffic drifting down the alleyway and through the slanted wooden door and the slow drip of a faucet. A steel coffee pot with Frisbees of green and grey surfing on black inside. A stolen newspaper box too full of garbage in the corner, a flag hung above it. A refrigerator with no magnets or flyers or coupons or photos. A table, one leg relying mostly on the others, green bottles against the wall underneath, two chairs, one with a tear in the orange padding. A toaster burnt from years of use. An open drawer and a large rat slumped still on its back on the counter next to a sink filled with dishes and a grey stained rag. He opened his eyes. Sleep blurred. The plastic, filthy blinds obscured the light. He took a shallow breath, coughed and closed them, rolling onto his back and craning his head to the right against the small stove, an ashtray tilting, wrapping the brown throw rug around himself as he went. A silent stream of sun slowly crept across the floor throughout the morning. As it reached his eyes, they watered and opened again, revealing the seven green bottles under the table whose leg he could not remember how he broke. He had been on the linoleum for the morning and part of the night before. Taking shaggy comfort on the brown carpet. He tried to close his eyes again. His eyelids throbbed in rhythm with his pulse, fast, made worse when he closed them tighter, clenched them. It was hot. He kicked the carpet until it was at his feet and rolled over again. He had no remnants of dreams left from his sleep and no memories from the night before quite yet, just confusion. He rolled and got to all fours, steadying himself, arm stretched should he fall towards the stove. A few heavy breaths and he was to his feet, looking across the yellow floor towards the short bathroom hallway. He stuffed his hand into his awkwardly folded pocket. No cigarettes but a lighter. He looked back at the ashtray on the floor and saw the cigarette butts. Collected, he lit the longest one and headed to the bathroom, unsure footing down the one stair. Briefly looking into the mirror, he turned on cold water after setting the lighter and three butts on the counter. He splashed some water into his mouth with his free hand and backed into the toilet and sat down, rubbed his eyes and pissed, dropping the cigarette butt between his legs. He lit another butt. Done, he stood up and threw the filter. There were seven filters floating in the toilet that was black with mold at the waterline. He turned towards the mirror. He didn't like it. His eyes were clear, given the night before, but his skin was haggard. Red hue over even redder lines on his cheeks and nose under the lines beside his eyes. Redness around the corners of his nose. A few red dots. A scar just below his hairline from where he had collided with a steering wheel years ago. He didn't remember how he got this old looking. He didn't remember how he got the cut on his cheek just above his beard. More of a deep scratch. He picked up the tube and folded toothpaste into his mouth, his hands under the cold water again shovelling into his mouth, swishing and onto his face. He spit and looked back towards the mirror. Something was smeared on his sweater. *Vomit?* It looked shiny. He unzipped it too fast and it caught, and he zipped an inch upwards and down again. Caught. He peeled it over his head in frustration, throwing it into the corner, and re-examined the mirror. Eye bags purple, hair matted with sweat yet wild tufts sprouting. He turned away towards the hallway.

He kept one eye open, the other closed, to see correctly. Slowly. He surveyed his surroundings. This was his place, the one he had rented for some time now, but he had never considered it his real home. More habit than anything else, he entered the kitchen. He noticed the bottle on the counter and instinctively took a drink, a strike against the headache that would surely be coming. He saw the glass that he had used the night before. Ashes inside but no butts. He rinsed it in the sink and wiped it with the brown rag, but then decided against it and took a cleaner one from the cupboard above. He poured from the green bottle, almost half a glass, and began to drink when he noticed the large black rat lying on his counter, it's bared front teeth yellowed, arms and legs curled. He coughed into the drink, splashing the whiskey into his nose and eyes, dropping the glass. He jumped backward. Shards burst outward while the base of the glass, spotty fangs upwards, ricocheted against the fridge and bounced behind his left foot just as he stepped downward. Panicked, he kicked his foot out in order to dislodge the glass that had pierced him but found it stuck for the first kick, caught in his sock, the second sending the remains of the glass into the stove. He dropped onto his back then up to his butt and looked at the sudden damage. The whiskey was burning the half inch long cut in the bottom of his foot. The cut didn't seem deep but started painfully at the crevice between his big and second toes, cutting the webbing and twisted around the side. He sat, holding his foot.

He rocked there, his foot wrapped in his bath towel, the other still draped in the grey sock he slept in, the other bloodied on the floor, at the edge of the tub. He tried to think of how long he'd been sitting there, blood still bubbling out. Had he been out of it? Sitting there, he began to realize how hot it was. And dry. He eventually rose and put pressure on his foot, the pain not as bad as he braced for. He opened the cabinet door under the sink. He found a clean cloth and the tensor bandage he had kept for years and bandaged his foot awkwardly, a tongue sticking out on either side of his big toe. He was sweating now. Alcohol and heat pouring out. He stood and made his way back to the kitchen, careful not to put too much pressure on his foot. Around the corner, he looked to his sink. There lay the rat. He went to the stolen newspaper box and opened it. The garbage can inside was full. Hc pulled it out, took the bag out of the office style garbage can and brought it to the door leading to the alley. Open. He noticed that the hinge had come loose again. Two months prior the hinge had been pulled out of the frame in frustration and he had used longer screws to reattach it. Now it had come loose again straining the bottom hinge enough that the crease in the metal was significantly lighter than the rest of the hinge. He threw the bag down the concrete steps and slammed the door. It didn't latch. Angrily, he pushed harder, reopened the door and re-slammed it causing one of the screws to drive back into the frame a bit and the other to pop out of the hinge nearly entirely. As he made his way back to the kitchen, he saw that he had left a sponged trail of blood to the bathroom and to the kitchen and to the door. Propping himself up on his left heel, he rubbed the floor with his foot. He spit on the floor and rubbed again, following his trail all the way back to the garbage can that occupied the center of his kitchen floor. He picked up the garbage can and went back to the rat on his counter. They weren't uncommon in the alley but he'd never had one in the house. Avoiding the glass, he pulled a dirty plate out of the sink, tilted the garbage can under the ledge of the counter and began to drag the rat towards the ledge. Suddenly, the rat squirmed onto its stomach, bouncing onto its hind legs. Again, he stumbled back in shock, nearly stepping onto another fractured slice. He steadied himself against the fridge and stared at the rat. He didn't run, just breathed, his body swelling unnaturally large with each inhale. The rat fell onto all fours, then hopped onto the floor and made its way towards him. Uncaring, un-nervously. He backed into the refrigerator as far as he could to give the rat a wide corridor in which to pass. It walked leisurely around the corner. He followed it as it made its way to the still open door that he was sure had latched, it turned around, stared again at him with its red eyes, no one, just a hole where the other should be. He walked towards the door as the rat jumped down the step but it was gone by the time he reached the doorway. He closed his eyes and shook his head to himself, shuffling back to sweep the glass.

There had been a fire burning far away from the city for a few weeks now, though today was one of the first days that the sky was noticeably greyer and smoky. Smoky enough to grey out the sun like a thin cloud.

There was no breeze, just the intense heat of summer devoid of any direct sunlight now that it was overcast. His wrapped foot barely fit inside his shoe though the pressure made it feel better than it had before. He picked up the bag of garbage from earlier in the day. Hours had passed since then. He had felt worse than he had even after finishing the rest of the bottle. He walked down the alley. Between the white door to the garage he spent most of the previous night in and the brown door leading to the kitchen of the diner next to his apartment. He tossed the bag he held by the knot at the red dumpster clumsily and it ripped against the rusty side, spilling its contents against the side of the building. Mostly bottles, a bunch of wet ashes and cigarette butts, unopened envelopes, coffee grounds, pill bottle, an empty cracker sleeve. He said nothing. He continued to walk down the alley towards the street. It smelled awful. Ashes and liquor. Something else he couldn't place. Something cooking, or even burning? Not the fire, not wood. Something else. He finally looked at his phone. He had noticed several unanswered texts and calls on his phone earlier but chose not to investigate. As he turned the corner out of the alley and down the street, he pressed the red numbers. Two calls were from his work. Two texts labelled Mom from the night before. Are you still coming tomorrow? And Call your mother please! He walked.

Yes ill be ther.

Not quite a block from the end of the alley, he entered the shop and bought two packs of cigarettes. Further down the street, the sign read 'Blues'. He lit a cigarette and took his phone out once again, picked a place to sit on the red brick ledge that had less burn and ash marks on it than the rest, against the window and pressed messages.

Hey…just wondering where you are; it's 8:20 already and we needed you today okaaaaaaaay, just, lemme know I guess.

To delete this message, press 7.

Oookaaay…you know what? Don't even bother coming in…thanks for the help today. I'll see you Monday.

He stood up and stepped towards the door but spun around. Thinking bullshit. He sat back down. It's at least 6; there is no way anybody is still there. Missed calls. A call back.

Hey it's me, I did not mean to screw you over today… I actually ended up in the hospital last night and I just left give me a call I guess if you are still there…sorry man.

The blue carpet he walked on after entering hadn't been new since the '70s and stuck slightly to his feet, if it could still be called carpet as the fibres had long since stood at the intended cushioning stance. The bar was vinyl and looked green with a white swirling pattern but had at one point been blue as well, now worn and polished from years of hands and elbows and foreheads and sleeves. He sat on a bar stool farthest from the door and ordered his drinks from the bartender he knew, though on this night he had acted like he didn't, hostile.

You look like shit, the bartender told him as he stepped to the back bar.

He faked a laugh. A single ha.

You can fuck yourself, you know that right? He slurred a little back.

The bartender gave no response, not verbal not facial, just poured the shot from the green bottle and a pint, spilling the pint slightly as he put the glass down, keeping his eyes on him and missing the coaster slightly offsetting the glass. He drank. The beer was warm. The television showing highlights waved and filtered downward with static. An older couple was sitting at a table near the window where he had sat. Out of the corner of his eye he thought they were staring at him.

It was around ten when he finally left. As he entered alley, the sky was darker than normal he thought, but the lights above the doorways lining the alley seemed brighter to him. He became preoccupied as he walked, with the bottle he had bought in his hand and a cigarette in the other that was carefully unscrewing the cap. Drunk and focused on the bottle, he never noticed the man who sat leaning against the brick facade.

Sir, can you spare any coin for an old guy, young brother?

Startled, he looked around before noticing the man a few feet to his left, completely visible in the alley lights yet camouflaged amongst the garbage that lined the alley. He wore dirty jeans that had holes in both knees and what appeared to be a grey sweater under a green winter jacket under a flannel autumn coat. He noticed that the man's shoes looked like his, only filthy and tattered, and that he hadn't shaved in what seemed like months, skin grey in the limited light. There appeared to be a dog cuddled under his arm only he couldn't see the dog's head. He squinted and tried to focus. There was something odd about his face he thought. Something very familiar. Normally, he was a talkative happy drunk, if not goofy, but lately, tonight, he had other things on his mind, he was angry.

Leave me alone, I got nothing, he told the man.

How about a smoke?

How about fuck off, he said louder, flicking the butt at his filthy shoes and dropping the lid to the bottle of whiskey in the process. The man said nothing, just watched him walk away. Disappointed look. He kept stumbling on down the alley towards his apartment, past the back door of the diner, past the filthy dumpster. The garbage from earlier was still scattered against the wall. He noticed the smell again, though stronger now. He wondered briefly if it was him. Past the garage that his rusted truck was stored in. He stopped and looked at the garage. He tried to think of the night before. *Did I try to drive?* He hadn't thought about it but now he had a feeling that he did something stupid. A feeling he would regret something. A feeling he was familiar with. He lifted the bottle to his lips but paused and instead turned away. He walked up the concrete steps; he saw that his door still wasn't properly shut, although again he thought he had closed it tightly. Maybe. He wasn't sure anymore. Without turning the knob, he pushed on the door heavily with his foot. It swung open easily and crashed into the wall behind it. He lifted the bottle halfway to his mouth, again to drink, but dropped it down again, almost letting it slip. It was dark inside. As he took a step in, he reached up to the left where he knew the light switch would be, where it had always been Pushing his hand slowly across the wall with his head down, his fingers felt the ridge of the plastic switch cover and leading to a bumpy surface. Not a switch. Too many ridges. *Bony?* His head jerked upwards and he recoiled as he recognized what he was rubbing were the knuckles on the back of someone's hand covering the switch. His head swelled as if he stood up too fast, a pulse of darkness. He felt the hand grab at his, trying to pull him into the darkness, snag his finger as he tugged, long nails scratching out at him as he screamed and twisted out of the door and down a stair, keeping his eyes fixed on the darkness as he retreated. Nothing. Blackness. He backed down the step, nearly falling, and into the alley never taking his eyes off of the doorway, trying to look inside using the light from the alley. There was no one there. He didn't move for a few seconds before going to the garage. He entered the code on the keypad on the wall, failing once before it began to open causing the lights above the door to automatically flicker then turn on. Peering through the window, under the throw he used as a curtain, it appeared that the living room was clear. He backed away, back into the light and looked at his hand. No scratches. Was he that drunk? He slowly made his way back up the stairs scanning as he went. He was more focused now and widened his eyes as if to clear any fog, opening his mouth as he did. He screamed.

Get the fuck out of my house!

Nothing once more. He stared again, hesitating a bit. Lighting his lighter as he stood in the doorway of the house, he could now see the switch, lunging at it to his left while ready at his right. His living room was clear. There was nowhere to hide in there. A single couch, a single chair, a wooden stand and a TV still surrounded by months of dust. A laptop on top of the coffee table that was badly damaged due to numerous spills. A blanket on the floor, a pillow on the couch. He walked quickly to the far wall and flipped on another switch. From there, he could see into the small bathroom. No one, the bathtub curtain was flipped over the curtain rod, a habit he had developed because of a former girlfriend. The door to the bedroom off of the living room also open. It looked empty. A little bit of light bounced through the living room into the bedroom and some light faded in from the other side of the apartment through the window. He slowly, quietly made his way around the corner, his stealth betrayed by groan of the floor. He held the bottle upright by his side, ready to use as a club if necessary, jumping into the kitchen, ready. There was no one there. *Did I actually imagine that?* he thought and quickly shuffled back around to the living room and into his bedroom doorway, noticing his torn foot as he did and using his heel the last few steps. His closet was open. He dropped to his hands and knees from a distance. Nothing under the bed except a shoebox and some sandals and some dirt. He got up and walked to the door again. Closed the garage door and went back up the concrete steps. Cautious still. He thought he heard laughter coming from the alley behind him. Maybe it was the bum watching behind him. He lit a cigarette and entered his home slamming the door closed behind him. Check the bathroom again. Nothing. There couldn't be he thought, unless someone stood in his sink. He went back to the kitchen and quickly grabbed a glass off of the counter and turned towards the living room. He looked at the glass, noticing it was the same one he had tried to wipe ash from in the morning, some still smeared around the inside of the base. He poured himself a finger as he sat on the couch, turning on the TV that only got basic cable. He didn't watch closely. He thought he heard a woman say something growly about fire. He noticed he was shaking some. He pulled the blanket over his lap and stared forward and sipped. He noticed the ash the whiskey tried to hide as it flaked towards his mouth

---

It was almost completely dark. The phone he kept upright on his lap had created light, pressing the on button every two minutes until he forgot about that. Now the faintest glow of red. He didn't keep track of time just stared ahead into nothingness. He closed his eyes and opened them. Not a blink, involuntarily slower. He felt nothing any more. *Wait. What's shaking? Am I shaking? No, something is vibrating. I don't like this.* He tried to get up but something was in the way. He felt metal and pushed and fell chin first onto something hard. *I don't like this* he thought again. *I don't want this.* He tried to crawl. Something was there watching him.

He groaned, and his arms lifted, thrashed. As his legs tensed they pushed on the arm of the couch, roped together and moving as one, shoving his torso close, then soon over the tipping point and sliding off of the couch, rolling, falling and hitting the ground solidly. Face first. He awoke in pain. Spun. He felt something beside him and, grabbing his nose, lifted himself up, his right eye connecting then with the rounded edge of the coffee table. He fell back and cringed. His hands covering his face and breathing heavy. He lay there, between the couch and the table, tangled in the blanket. Slowly, eventually, he looked between his fingers, holding them like a target, and knew where he was. It was a nightmare. He laughed a bit. Not quite honest but almost. He put his hands on top of his head and turned it to the right. Through the table top and the smaller stained shelf underneath he could see his door. *Actually closed* he thought. He stayed for a while, thinking of the dream. He remembered being confined. *What was the dream about? Something was shaking me?* He carefully lifted himself. His eyes met the glass from the night before. Black flecks on a tiny lake of gold. He didn't debate, just lifted, left arm pushing up on the couch, right hand allowing the flow into his mouth, he steadied himself as he stood, while he lifted each leg in turn to loosen the blanket. He placed the glass behind him on the table and picked up his phone. It was dead, but the grey twilight coming through the bottom of the throw he had tacked onto the wall around the window instead of a curtain told him it was early. He slipped out of the rest of his blanket restraint and turned towards his bedroom. Turning back, he grabbed the blanket then walked to the bed. He thought that it felt like forever since he felt his mattress. He flopped. He remembered the phone was dead and grasped blindly at the side of the mattress where it should be, coming up with nothing, eventually peaking over the side and spotting the cord. Plugged. He turned his head away and closed his eyes.

Urururuuruuruuruururuuruuruuru

He could feel it vibrate.

Urururururuuurururur

Two.

Urururururuuurururur

He rolled back over. Three missed texts.

Urururururuururuuurur

Four. The screen told him 'MOM' was the last one. It also read 10:22. He stared and then stood, not reading the texts but figuring it out. Quickly looking at the closet, he opened a drawer and pulled out underwear and socks, socks lightly holed with age and the shirt his mom had got him months before for his birthday. He scanned the floor and found jeans. These ones had a large smear on the front. He looked at the pair he had on still. They seemed clean. He walked towards the bathroom. Tossing his clothes onto the floor he turned and pulled on the shower knob, pulled the curtain down, shed the ones he still had on, not careful to separate the ones he was wearing and the ones he would wear and walked back to the living room. He spied his cigarettes and pink lighter on the table. Grabbing them, he didn't know where he got a pink lighter from. Back to the toilet. He sat back down, lit a cigarette and decided to let the water warm up while he waited. Calmed, looking down now. The grey sock on one foot and the brown cloth tightened with the tensor under the sock on the other. He pulled the sock off. He began to unravel the tensor. He hadn't noticed any pain since he searched the place yesterday but now he felt it. Throbbing. With each twist, more and more burgundy, dried blood, until the cloth fell. He examined his foot. A cut still raw. Too raw. Pink radiating and fading onto his toes. It hurt now more than it did before. Standing up, he looked into the fogging mirror. The scratch just above his beard looked worse. Scabbed now but wider. His eye. Red forming under it. He scratched his head and swept away the curtain.

He sat on the end of the bed. Shoes on already, cut double socked, he pulled on the shirt and his black jacket that had the torn right inside pocket he was careful not to put anything inside. He thought about his parents and lamented what was to come. He had always been close with his mother and father but ever since the accident, it had been strained. They had blamed him for what had happened to his son. He didn't disagree. He checked his pockets and counted to five: wallet, phone, cigarettes, lighter…Wait…he counted again: wallet, phone, cigarettes, lighter…he groped his pockets, searching, before finding the fifth. He pulled his keys from his back left pocket that was full of change as well from the night before. He recounted and made his way to the door, stopping to pick up the bottle on his way. He stopped though, and put the bottle down. He left and closed the door, positive it was closed when he slammed it. He pressed 1 5 0 5 on the keypad. Just a beep. 1 5 0 5. The door opened, slowly, with purpose. He didn't duck under as it lifted as he normally would but waited, eventually revealing the desk in the corner covered in sparse tools, a half missing ratchet set, a hammer, a plastic container that held most of the essentials for hanging framed pictures of your loved ones, a few random screwdrivers, a utility knife and a length of eavesdrop drainage pipe on the floor, bent into a crude arch. He looked at the pipe and kicked it aside and opened the truck, realizing it had come off the side of the garage but unable to remember why it was no longer serving its purpose. It wasn't quite closed, only halfway. He got in and turned the key. The music started with a screech, several guitars singing a high note. Startled, he punched the stereo at the volume button. The screech was now accompanied by a buzz. He turned it off. He couldn't remember having the music that high. He didn't like the music that loud. He turned the key. It turned over but wouldn't start. Again, same result. Third time it sputtered to life. It shook, convulsing a bit, just enough for him to see that the gauge read E. It died again. He tried again. Punch the horn. Heavy breath. Okay, he thought. He opened the door pressed the button attached to the sun visor and ducked under before the garage door closed. He went back inside the apartment. He stood in the center of the hall for a bit but then went to the table, looked at the bottle, turned and made his way out of the door. Frustrated. He slammed the door several times. Today is Saturday he thought.

He sat. Bouncing. The brown seat concealing springs that had long since decided they had served their purpose and retired. He tried to forget why he was riding the bus across the city to his parents' house. It smelled. Piss and ash. He pulled his phone out of his pocket. 4 texts now.

You're still coming right sweetie?

Let us know if you need a ride okay?

Then unexpectedly:

Hey, how's things?

Listen you should call me, okie?

He read and reread the last two several times…

The jerking bus didn't wake him but rather an elderly lady pushing down on his toe with her brass tipped stick as she walked towards the front of the bus. He reacted in pain, pulling his foot out from under the spear and out of the aisle, but stopped himself from yelling as he realized what had happened. She looked back at him, crudely wrinkled face showing no remorse. He looked up and recognized the name that tickered across the orange and black screen. Oaky St. He had gone too far, maybe a few blocks he thought. He followed the woman and several others off of the bus. Onto the sidewalk. The street was lined with businesses, small brick and plaster buildings that he didn't recognize. A small defunct lumber company, a pawn shop, a vacuum and small engine repair business that looked abandoned for decades if not for the open sign hanging on the door, framed by bare grey wood that had long since lost its paint. The sky was greyer today. Greyer and hotter. He wondered how close he was right then to the fire that was consuming the countryside and hills. He tried to light a cigarette as he began walking and pivoted around and faced the bus stop, walking backwards as he did in order to shield his lighter from the breeze that didn't exist. As he did, he glanced up at the people that had left the bus with him. Most seemed old, too old, and he thought that most were looking in his direction. All were looking in his direction. Some walked slowly towards him, some standing rigidly. Looking at him. Beyond him. Dressed in suits and dresses, Sunday finery. A lone young boy wearing a blue and yellow baseball uniform. He turned and walked faster than normal, pulling his phone out of his pocket. It told him he was six blocks away.

You're late you know, his father accused him.

Yep, I'm aware.

Your mother is napping; don't slam the door.

He said nothing. He followed his father to the kitchen, past the hallway and the door to the room he slept in for 17 years of his life that held posters and girlfriends and trophies and pot and memories, past the stairway that led to the basement where he played Legos and barbies with his older sister and they would sneak down and watch movies late at night, cartoons and comedies and westerns, without their parents knowing even though they knew. Past the photos of them, as a family, throughout the years when they were happy, through childhood and teenage years and graduations and sickness. Past the painting of rocks and a dirt road his grandmother had painted because it reminded her of her childhood before she was struck with cancer and passed. Past the ceramic bear with the barely noticeable glued on head that sat in front of photos that his sister had made in 6th grade and gave her mother on mother's day that were grouped together on top of the darkly stained wooden pedestal that his father loved but his mother secretly hated and that he had cut his head on after he had been pushed as a child by his sister, afterwards promising each other they wouldn't tell dad. He had been past these things many times and yet it seemed to him it was the first time he ever really saw them. He sat at the table he ate at as a child as his father pulled a saran covered plate from fridge. The table where he made his parents proud and disappointed. Where he was scolded and praised. Where he was asked to come home and told to leave. His father put what looked a piece of casserole into the microwave then sat at the table. Neither noticed the faint smudge of blood he left behind.

So your mother was looking forward to seeing you today, his father said.

I know…my truck wouldn't start this morning… I actually think it was out of gas but I managed to park it so I don't know how.

How do you run out of gas?

I don't know, Dad. It wasn't a well thought out plan. I wasn't even low when I got home on Thursday…Friday. Maybe kids broke in and siphoned it.

He shook his head sarcastically as he said this but realized at the same time that his garage had been broken into before and that actually could have happened.

Kay, his dad shook.

The microwave beeped it's annoying three beeps and his father went to a drawer and pulled out a fork, then took what he now saw was Shepard's pie from the microwave. His father brought it to him but after he placed the china down as one would normally, he dropped the fork down and it bounced off of the table cloth, almost off the table. He moved it to the plate.

I assume this has nothing to do with your face, right?

He closed his eyes and breathed deeply, keeping a smile on his face as he did before looking back at his father.

These are actually separate incidents believe it or not, he explained. I managed to hit myself in the face with a screwdriver while fixing my door yesterday, he lied. And I rolled off the couch sleeping this morning and managed to smack my eye off the table when I went to got up, he said truthfully.

His father looked down and nodded as he scooped some food into his mouth, the first he had had in…he couldn't remember.

And I assume work is going well, no problems there?

He wondered quickly if his father could possibly know about yesterday, wondered whether he had caught him saying Thursday before catching himself and replacing it with Friday. He weighed his options.

It's fine, he lied and paused. It's work I guess I don't know. I still hate it but I show up, he said. A truth and a lie.

His father stood up and went to the cupboard and as he did, he scooped more of the corn and potato and beef into his mouth. He hadn't felt hungry in a day or two and sill didn't. His father poured himself a drink, in view of his son, and walked back to the table. He placed the drink in front of himself, but placed it down deliberately, presenting it.

You want a drink?

No, Dad, he said, another lie, but a conflicting one.

Have you been to see your sister?

He looked down and ate another forkful.

Not for a week, Dad, he said through corn.

Why?

Because…because I don't like seeing her li— He was interrupted.

You think she wants to be there?

He thought about standing, leaving. He put his fork down. Sarcastically, he said, No, Dad, I don't think my sister likes seeing herself have cancer. What are y— Cut off again.

Shut the Fuck UUUUUUPP!

He stood up and backed into the pedestal. He didn't know where this burst had come from. He had never seen his father mad. His eyes were wild. Not with anger. With hate, it seemed.

Calm down. I'll go see her tomorrow. It's okay.

No it fucking isn't okay.

We can go right now if you want.

You know what, I don't want to see you right now. Get out.

He didn't respond for a few seconds. You're serious, he said, I'm going to hug Mom first.

His father pushed him by the chest, almost to the ground but instead hit the door.

Get the fuck out! Get out now!

He turned. Fuck you. He left.

He hadn't noticed the ash coming down when he left his place this afternoon, not until he had turned the corner onto the street that led to his alley that led to his apartment. It ambushed him. He had been sweating in the evening sun and the ash clung to him in grey streaks and slashes. He hadn't noticed. He had been replaying the afternoon's events in his mind. Going over every detail. Wondering why today would be the day his father would snap. Wondering what had set him off. Wondering when he would hug his mother again. Wondering when he should visit his sister, whether she would want him to, but knowing she would. He hadn't noticed his shirt becoming greyer, that the neckline was colouring his throat a darker grey. He kept his head low, focusing on the sidewalk, focusing on each individual seam in the concrete. He didn't notice that he was leaving marks on the concrete behind him. Each step more deliberate than the last, each one a step closer to being at his apartment again, a step closer to his mattress and pillows and quilt his grandmother had created for him years before. He hadn't noticed that there was only his footprints in the ash he left behind, as if he had been walking in snow, or that this particular street was abandoned except for himself. He hadn't noticed the wind picking up, the first breeze he had felt in days. He hadn't noticed until he had turned the corner and a rush burnt its way into his throat, threatening to choke him. He coughed. As he coughed, his eyes watered. As his eyes watered, the soot that had gathered in the folds of his eyelids liquefied and burned its way into him. He rubbed his blackened eyes with his blackened hands, then pulled his shirt over his eyes in desperation. He stayed like that, hunched on the sidewalk, in the ashes. He stayed in that position, afraid to remove the shirt from his cheeks should it allow more ash into his eyes. Pressing the cotton into his eyes gave him a sense of safety, even as he braced himself to see again. It was now he noticed how much his foot hurt. He hadn't felt the scab strain and loosen and eventually break apart as he walked. Now he could. He pulled the shirt away from his eyes, looking down at his feet to no end and seeing the bright red mark on his grey shirt, unsure of how long he had been bleeding from the face, from the scab on his cheek that he still had no explanation for. It was now he realized the fire had to be getting closer to the city, that there were ashes snowing down upon him. It was now he realized he was alone. He strained and looked behind him, to see a face, any face, anything to let him know that he wasn't abandoned though now he was. He scanned the sidewalk. He did not see any footsteps. He scanned the ashes on the street. He did not see any tire marks. He told himself, reassured himself, that the falling ash had simply hidden any marks that were there, that it was too dark to see them. Something out of the corner of his eye caught his attention. Someone was there, though not on the street, but staring at him out of the window to their second story home. A woman. Glaring. And another. A man a few windows down. Same expressionless look on his face that the woman had. Expressionless, yet somehow glaring. Hatefully. He turned his head and walked, wanting to conceal his view of the two just as soon as to be out of view of the two. A light chill came over him and left just as quickly. He wiped his face on the shirt once more. Just a few blocks away now. Just one or two stops before home. Just one. Maybe two.

He could see his door open again. This time with purpose, it seemed. Someone had surely been inside his place. He thought about the garage. What he could use if someone were still inside. 1-5-0-5. The light flickering on and the garage door opening slowly, slower than normal, then stopping altogether about 5 feet up. No time. He ducked into the room, past his truck, past the bent piece of gutter and to the bench. He picked up the yellow plastic that had the thin rusted metal revealing itself from the end. He twisted the knob to force more of the blade out but it had become rusted into place after neglect and carelessness. Ducking back under the door, he made his way to the window. No sign of anyone, just a red light on his laptop. He tried to remember if he had closed the door that morning. He had slammed it he thought. He was sure of it. Now it was wide-open, inviting, waiting for him. He made his way to the stairs. There was ash in the doorway spreading itself out a few feet into the place. No footsteps. He strained to see inside. He thought about the events earlier in the afternoon. He could have sworn he had slammed the door but never thought to make sure it was properly closed. Now, looking in with the dim help of the flickering light outside, he was no longer sure of himself. He didn't turn on the light. Slowly, he positioned himself inside the living room so that he could see into his bedroom and the bathroom. There was no one there. Around the corner. The kitchen was empty. Nowhere to hide. He looked into the bathroom again down the hall. The curtain was still draped over the top of the rod as he had left it in the morning. His towel still on the floor concealing a bloody rag and bloody tensor underneath. He walked to his bedroom. Like he had the day before, he dropped to his knees outside of the room in case someone should be under the bed. A shoebox, some sandals, some dirt. Closet still open. He rose and went back to the door, pulling out his cigarettes as he went. He sat on the crumbling step and lit his lighter. A puff of sour smoke entered his lungs as the filter caught fire in a burst of green. He tried to spit the cigarette out but the paper stuck on his lip just enough to dangle helplessly before falling onto his lap. He swatted it away, throwing his pink lighter as he did, several feet away and directly in front of the large one-eyed rat. Startled by the appearance of his companion, he bounced. *What in the fuck?* The rat calmly smelled the cigarette before turning his attention to the lighter that had surrounded itself in the ash, then back to the cigarette. He watched. The rat didn't recoil from the smoke rising into its face. Instead it stayed, smelling the burnt cotton cylinder as it smouldered, the last wisp floating into his sole red eye. Slowly, he picked up a small chunk of concrete that had come loose from the step. Carefully, he took aim at the rat and threw. The chunk glanced of off the pavement bouncing through the ash, taking some speed off of it, and over the rat. It tripped a bit, attempting to get its footing after the surprise, before running down the alley, past the homeless man from the evening before, sitting in the same spot, a little dirtier, a little ashier, than the previous night. He didn't know why he had done that. He was angry at the events of the day, at his father, at himself, but not the rat. The rat was just a rat, had nothing consequential about it, and yet he found himself hating the rat as well. He went to the garage door and tried to pull it closed. The motor above had quit and he couldn't pull it down manually. Frustrated. He left the door open, light on outside. He approached the homeless man, still wearing the same flannel and sweater and coat. Still wearing the shoes that were the same as his. Face dirtier than the day before. He looked gaunter, his eyes more sunken somehow. Darker. Yet strangely familiar. Recognizable eyes.

Hey, weird question, have you been here all day? Like since around three or so?

I don't generally keep the time young man, he said looking down at his bare wrist.

Sure, kay, did you see anyone go in there? he said pointing to the door.

A woman came by here earlier.

Did she go inside?

I don't know.

You don't know?

I don't know.

Cool. Fuck, thanks, he said sarcastically.

She was crying.

What?

The old woman. She looked sad. She was crying when she left. Got a cigarette?

She was an old crying woman?

Older. You got a cigarette on you?

No, he lied.

He turned and walked back to his door. As he did, he saw his footprints, looping around the front of the garage and into the apartment, and a second set, a set he hadn't noticed before, more visible at first then gradually fading from view as he neared the door. Filled in with ash, he thought. The ash that still stung his eyes. Someone had been there.

He poured warm water from his bathroom faucet into a large bowl that had previously held popcorn and hadn't been cleaned, and brought it to the living room, pushing the coffee table out of the way with his foot and placing the bowl on the floor. He turned the television on but turned his attention to his foot. Blood had seeped through both layers of sock during his walk during the day and had stained the bottom of both socks maroon. He peeled them off of his foot simultaneously, careful to pry from the bottom and pull down rather than pulling from the tip, revealing the wound. It had tried to heal during the night it seemed but tore back open during the day. Freshly dabbed and mottled blood framed by a dark, almost black attempt to repair itself. He dipped his foot in the water, immersed. It stung, but he kept it there as the pain melted away and became soothing. The news was on again. He grabbed the remote. Sports. A movie from 1985 that he would enjoy if he actually watched it. People arguing on a beach on a channel that used to play music. History of the North African campaigns of the Second World War. He left it there. He reached into the bowl and cradled some water out, splashing it on his face and down his shirt. He looked at his phone again.

Listen you should call me, okie?

He thought for a while. He hadn't seen a friendly text come from this number in years. Not a sincere one. He wondered whether or not this text was truly friendly or feigned and phony. He texted. Talking to her always reminded him of his son and so he stopped. He thought of his son now. The car accident. He would be a few months away from going to high school now. He couldn't actually remember the accident itself. Only waking up in the hospital. Waking up and being told the news. Being told the news by an angry wife and family. Being told it was all his fault before she stomped out of the room. They were divorced a few months later. And he had been here ever since.

What do you want? I'm home now if you want to call.

He sat, awaiting a reply, watching the Desert Fox himself pushing into Egypt.

He laid on the floor, struggling to breath. He couldn't remember why. He had managed to open and close the door before falling into a slimy puddle. It was still cold. It felt nice on his face. It smelled awful in the alley. He was hot. *Where am I?* He tried to look around but his eyes were blurred with tears and instability. He was being watched. He couldn't see but he could feel. He looked up. Shapes. *No not blurry. Smokey?* He had an audience. More than one, led by the largest. He pushed himself to his hands and knees and started to crawl. He could feel the hand on his ankle, clawing, burning, trying to hold him in place, losing its grasp but still content now just following him, watching him, judging him. Howling. Not human. No not human. Something worse. Something angry with him. It wanted to show him something he was sure he did not want to see. Something much worse. No. Not human. *You're not real. You can't be real.*

He woke up, hot, sweating, struggling to breath. It was black. Where am I, he thought, briefly. He could see a faint outline of the door. He thought he could see the TV flicker but was unable to lift his head to see. He wasn't alone he thought. What is that? Something stood in his living room, staring at him through the doorway. He tried to cry out, to yell at it. He couldn't. *Please leave me alone. Please leave.* The thing came closer, watching him. It had no eyes but it could see, no form yet visible. Coming towards him but not on legs. He struggled. He struggled to move, to roll over. He struggled to sit up, to get away from this thing. *Get up!* His hand moved. He blinked. He tried to yell out again, lips moving but no words. Nervousness and dread. His legs twitched. Slowly coming closer, past the frame and nearing the end of the bed. He tried to shake his head. No. Breathing heavier now, heavier still, panicked, eyes not moving from the thing though unable to make it out. A murmur escaped, faint. It moved like fog, like smoke. No eyes, pits. No mouth. Just anger. His head began to rock back and forth. His fingers moved. His knees and legs tensed lightly.

Go, he whispered.

Now hovering above him.

Go, he said.

The fog moved closer to his face still. The shadow.

Go, he yelled. Go! He sat up in bed. Go!

Staring at the doorway, he realized he was alone, realized what had happened. It was the same as before, same as dozens of times, yet different. They called them night terrors. Sleep paralysis. Normally, a woman. A witch. She would pay him a visit every couple of months, just to watch him, to scare him. And he would lay paralyzed. Unable to yell out. And she would sit upon his chest and squeeze him. Pushing on his lungs until he thought he would suffocate before pulling her long finger tips out of his chest and allowing him to breath, to yell at her, to make her leave and then simply fade out, never there to begin and leaving him unable and unwanting to return to sleep. This was different. He got up and went to the living room, to the window. He couldn't remember going to bed. His garage door was still open. He pulled on a set of pyjama pants, the blue ones he had a received from his sister on his birthday 6 months ago, and the slippers that unintentionally matched. Smoke lit. His door was closed now tightly. He jerked on the handle. It didn't move. He tried again, frustrated. A groan but no movement. He punched the door now, and again harder. Breath. Don't lose it. He lifted up on the brass as he turned the knob and pulled. It opened. The ashes that had rained during the day had stopped. Maybe the wind changed direction, he thought though he couldn't feel any wind. He could still see his footsteps from the day before, grinding the grey ash into heavy black smudges on the step, in front of the garage. No sign of the other footsteps. He saw that ash had made its way into the garage peppering the brown floor. He walked back into the house and into the kitchen, pulled the broom from behind the green newspaper box, then stopped. He went to his fridge. He hadn't eaten more than a few bites over two days though he wasn't hungry. He noticed what appeared to be red sauce on the handle then came to see it as more blood, somehow climbing up from his foot or down from his face. Opening the fridge, he saw condiments. Ketchup, mustard, hot sauce, barbecue sauce. He saw pickles and olives and expired milk and ginger ale he had bought a month ago to mix his whiskey with but never using it. He saw bread. He pulled the loaf out and put his slices in the burned toaster. He went back to the door and outside to the garage. 1-5-0-5. Still nothing. He tried to pull the door down. Nothing but the sound of metal scraping against metal as the chain to the motor strained under his weight. He pushed upwards. It moved. He shoved upwards now, sure to fling the door completely open. It remained slightly closed. He pushed it with the broom to the level of the frame. He looked at the ground in front of him and began to sweep, sure to use a light touch, pulling the ash towards him with purposeful strokes, starting from the right. A few feet in he saw it. A stain in front of the truck. He didn't remember why the stain was there, or why it was important, but somehow he knew he would find it there as if whispering to him, whispering a secret. Soap? It had dried with the appearance of being wet. Glossy, yet bubbled. Light green. Had he seen the stain in his dream he thought. Or maybe he had simply saw it the day before. He couldn't remember the dream. Only that he was scared. He stared at it for a time, unsure why, before turning back towards the door. He wondered if the homeless man still sat in the alley. When he returned to the kitchen, his toast was complete. In the dark, he reached for a knife but settled on a spoon and went about smearing the butter that sat on his counter. He wondered if the rat had gotten into it. He took a bite of one of the pieces. He coughed. Dusty and sour. He groped the darkness above his head and found the chain. Mold. The bread was blue, spotted, visible beneath the colour of the toasting, shiny with butter. He coughed again, spitting into the sink. He took the same glass he had used two days prior, filled it from the faucet, and drank, repeating the process. He sighed now, standing over moldy toast that lay accusingly on his counter. He picked it up and threw it against the wall in one movement. It dropped pathetically to the table. He opened the fridge. Examining, he saw it now, he hadn't noticed before, but he saw it now. Saucers of green and blue and white scattered amongst the bottles. Pickles blackened. Milk scum dried onto the side of the plastic. He felt the rack. Warm. The smell of rot hitting him now. The same smell. He opened the freezer. A bottle he forgot was there. He placed his hand against it. Warm. Almost hot. He removed the bottle from the freezer and closed the doors, turning his back to them. Pulling the chain again, he let himself slide down and onto the floor, pushed his hands against his face, and began to cry. Outside, the light above the garage door flickered briefly then died.

There was a gas station about ten blocks away, he thought. He had spent the rest of the early morning on the kitchen floor, awake, slowly sipping from the bottle he had found but he didn't feel intoxicated. He felt tired.

The sun burned through the window and the ash that dusted it. It felt hot on his face. He hated it but had refused to move, something he could control, just closed his eyes and allowed a few dim rays to filter through his eyelids. He had things to do today that he didn't want to. He checked his phone. Three missed calls last night from a familiar number and one text.

Sorry I was busy.

He hadn't heard it ring. He had expected a message from his mother but no. He typed.

I'm sorry I missed you yesterday. Call me.

He hadn't showered, instead wiping his face and neck and arms and genitals with a dish rag before changing his clothes and putting on a hat. He sat on the bed for a while. His foot, triple socked this time, throbbed worse than before, as did his face. He had refused to look in a mirror, to look at the cut and his eye. He didn't care about that. Brace yourself. You got this. He counted while he felt his pockets, 1, 2, 3, 4, 5, and headed out of his bedroom. He looked at his shoes resting by the crease in the slightly open door. Ashes. He forced them onto his feet. Laces tied. He struggled with both, smudging the ashes. He thought for a moment they looked like the bums shoes. Funny. When he left he didn't bother slamming the door. The ash was thicker now. He wondered again how close the fire must be. How hot. Ducking under the door that he didn't need to duck under, he went to the back of the truck and loosened the cord he had tightened himself years ago, when he lived in the countryside, from the small jerry can in the back of the truck. He ducked again. He saw that the stain had been covered by ash again. Footprints gone. He walked. That smell of something burning was back. Not wood. He gagged a little imperceptibly.

As he turned the corner down the street he felt a blast. A furnace. Stifling. His alley must have kept the wind out he thought. He briefly closed his eyes to shield them from the wind. He didn't notice the swirling mass of heat and ash whipping down the sidewalk towards him until it hit him, danced around him briefly, furiously, then died as quickly as it had been born. He coughed.

Fuck off, he whispered, to nothing.

The street was deserted. He didn't mind that today. He had no desire to see faces today, even those of strangers, let alone those he knew. He wasn't feeling the effects of the alcohol still yet had an anxiousness about him he hadn't felt in years. Impending. No, something looming. He began to walk faster. Anything to quicken the trip and get the day over with as soon as possible, to be alone again. To be able to hide.

The cashier hadn't been particularly nice. *Of course,* he thought, *I must look like shit.* The little can of gasoline was heavy. He wondered how hot the air would have to be to ignite it, to cause it to burst in his hands. He turned into the alley. The bricks gave him a small breather from the heat. Breath. As he walked he saw that the bum didn't sit there this morning. He hadn't thought about this when he left but now saw that the imprint of where he had been leaning against the brick the night before looked fresh. *Did I not notice the man when I left?* The wind should have filled in the indent by now, consumed it, but there it was, contoured and black between the random debris. He kept on, making sure to confirm the door to his place was still closed, and into the garage, not careful to strap the can back down after he filled the truck, throwing it into the back. He got in. After a few tries the engine caught and vibrated. He looked up and bent the mirror towards his face. He studied. The scratch on his cheek had turned into a cut overnight, still being attacked on all sides by black scab but not healing. His eyes were immersed in dark pools, especially the right. Redness painted his face in splotches. He thought he looked older than ever. He felt like this often after a session of drink that lasted a few days. He told himself this will all pass. He told himself it wouldn't pass soon enough. Couldn't pass soon enough. To his right, on the floor, a green bottle rolled and shifted as he pulled into the alley. Reflexively, he reached behind him and opened the window to the box of the truck and dropped the bottle through it. It shattered.

Fuck off, he said to no one.

A man ran past the front of his truck as he entered the parking lot. He seemed scared, as if he was running from something. He couldn't see what. The arm lifted as he took a ticket from the little box. He drove slowly into the parking lot. The rush he was in to get the day's events out of the way earlier had given way to a need to avoid it as long as possible. As the truck idled in the parking lot he examined himself in the mirror again. No changing this now. Up the steps. He hated this place. Nothing but memories of death. The large glass doors hesitated but opened for him. There was no need to stop at the receptionist's desk. He knew where he was heading. He thought she glared at him as well. Same look the cashier had given him earlier. The smell of disinfectant mingled with the burning that had drifted in from outside. The doors he passed were numbered, faded pink numbers on faded cream doors and walls, filled with people whose names he would never know. Filled with machines he didn't know the functions of or how they worked. Filled with soap and blood and syrups and shit. Next hallway. He wondered if she would be lucid today. Often times the combination of her medication and the illness made her unable to speak. Unable to comprehend who he was or her surroundings or why she was there, unable to move. He made his way to her door, breathing heavily as he did, and entered. It was dark in the room. Someone had drawn the curtains and failed to turn on a light. He could see her outline on the bed. He looked towards the windows. They were covered with a thick curtain to keep light out which he opened then and sat down beside her. She looked worse than he had ever seen her. She hadn't looked this pale. She hadn't had a machine breathing for her. She had an IV piercing her arm but it looked foreign now He took her hand. It was cold. Icy. Years ago when he was first told about her condition, the doctors had given them hope. Had given them reason to believe that in time everything would be fine. Later, she had beaten it. She was well until months ago and now here she was dead to the touch and eyes if not for the machine proving otherwise to him. He put his head on the bed and held her hand.

It was the scariest thing he had ever experienced. He had woken in the night unable to move. He never had a night light growing up, rather his parents would leave the hall light on and his door cracked. This night, the light was turned off as he lay in the black, paralyzed. This was the first time he had met the witch. Lying in the black but still able to see her clearly, creeping towards him, floating. It was the first time she had slowly pierced his chest with her long claws, growling at him, hissing. It was this night he woke up screaming in his bed, after she had gone, in the black. It was his sister who burst through the door to save him, who calmed him down and hugged him until his mother arrived. Saved him from his first night terror. He began to cry. This should be him, he thought. She was a better person than him. *This should be me.* He held her hand for an hour, watching her eyelids. They were still. A siren was yelling outside the window.

He wanted to, but he didn't stop at the receptionist to ask her any questions about his sister. He didn't ask to speak to her doctor. After a few hours, he didn't know how long, he just left. Let go of her hand and did not look back. He just wanted to go home. Go home and lie down on his mattress. Lie down and try not to think of anything. Try not to think of memories of his sister. Try not to think of his parents. Or his work the next day. Try to ignore the throbbing that had taken over his foot. It was late in the day now and getting darker, the ash that floated obscuring the moon. As he entered the parking lot he saw the cause of the alarm. A car had been in an accident and had been abandoned in the far corner of the parking lot. Still pushing into the other car, its red paint smeared into the black of the other. He ran to the edge of the lot to investigate. Crumpled pieces of plastic and shattered orange and clear glass littered the area surrounding the accident. *Whoever had been in this accident was hurt, they must have been going fast*, he thought. *Why hadn't the police come? And the alarm been shut off?* He moved over to the black car that was pinned between the concrete divider and the other car. The black tire marks that lay streaking through the ash divided themselves around a small pool of blood that looked fresh through the ever-growing covering of grey that was drifting down. *What in the fuck is going on,* he thought. He was the only person in the parking lot he realized. There were plenty of cars in the parking lot. Plenty of cars that looked like they had been there for some time judging by the ash blanketing them. There was no one on the sidewalk on the other side of the street either. The buildings on that side were caked in ash. Suddenly, an intense worry came over him. He began to panic. It felt like someone was watching him. He felt like a child again, overcome with anxiety at the thought of having to deliver a speech in front of the class. He began to feel dizzy and ran for his truck, fumbling with his keys while he attempted to open the door. Inside now. Lock the door. He tried starting the truck, turning over but not starting. Searching the parking lot around him, the wind seemed to come out of nowhere, pushing light brown and grey ash down the street as he tried again, successfully. As he left the parking lot, the panic, anxiety disappeared almost as soon as it had come on, though his heart still beat rapidly. *Get it together man,* he thought, and breathed a slight laugh.

The street his parents' home was off of was coming up. He thought about stopping by his parents' place, just to say hi to his mother, tell her he loved her and that he was sorry about the day before. To see his father and let him know about his sister's condition, that she was worse. To tell her about his nightmares over coffee while he watched TV. However, he kept driving past the street he needed when it presented itself. He felt ashamed as he did.

The show he was watching hadn't interested him. His intention had been to go home and not think of his sister. He had bought a large green bottle and cigarettes on his way home to help. Not think of her and sleep. Sleep and not dream. Not dream of the horrible things he had in the last couple of nights. He had taken two blue pills when he returned home in order to calm himself from the thoughts he couldn't escape yet they had barely taken effect. He had turned on his favorite TV show earlier. Hours later, he couldn't tell you which episodes he had watched. Or how many. He had drunk what was left in the bottle he had discovered the night before. About half. Another glass now in his hands. Blurry. He checked his phone. Nothing. He went to his texts and pressed dad. He wrote.

Hey, I just want you to know that I love you, you and Mom, and that I went to see her today. I don't know what you guys know. She looked worse. I didn't know she was on the breathing thing. Call me tomorrow and we can head back after work or whatever.

He stared at what he had written. He was angry. Wanting to press send but suddenly unwilling to be the first to do so. He turned it off without. He stood. He went outside, door sticking slightly, sat on the concrete and lit a cigarette. Placing his glass on the step, a gust of wind swirled and dropped ash neatly on top of the liquid where it briefly floated before dancing to the bottom of the glass. He noticed now that the light from the garage had burnt out, the halogen type he didn't keep a spare of. *Who would?* He looked down the alley. He thought he could see that the homeless man was back, a faint orange glow heaving brighter every few seconds. At least someone gave him a cigarette. He tried to focus on the cigarette, taking long, purposeful puffs. He tried to smoke in unison with the man in the alley but he was going too fast, breathing it rather than smoking it seemed. He thought of a tower beacon. Or a lighthouse. He was sleepy. The pills had taken effect quicker than they should have. Eyes closed. He hadn't bothered cleaning up his place this afternoon. The rotting condiments still stationed in his fridge. Moldy toast still where he threw it. Bloody socks and rags and tensors still on the floor of the bathroom. He inhaled periodically until he could feel the heat of the ember on his fingers. He got up and headed inside, casually tossing his cigarette into the ash as he did, slamming the door tight and back to the couch to not watch his show. Not watch his show in the light of the lamp that was on in his room, being ignored. After a few minutes, the TV flickered slightly, asking for his attention. He thought about turning the TV off and reading one of the books that still sat in the cardboard box in his room closet. And again. *I see you TV, what do you want.* He checked his phone instinctively, not expecting any messages or calls and expecting correctly. And again. *Now you're annoying me.* There had been three calls earlier. Three calls from someone he hadn't seen in a long time and refused to admit that he wanted to. The sound of static began to fade in and out, slow at first then quicker. The picture disappeared.

God, fuckING, dammit!

He got up to inspect. As he looked behind the television, he realized he didn't know what he was looking for. Two cords going in and one going out to the wall. There was a knock on the door, three separate strikes. He didn't respond. Just started. Three more. Louder now.

Hello?

No response. Three more again. He could feel them. He spied through the window, trying to see someone. He couldn't. Three more, louder still, shaking the door.

Who the fuck is it!

No response. He thought.

If that's you, you fucking bum, I'll fucking kill you!

He started to panic. No response. Three more again, loudest yet. He could feel them in his chest. He felt like they were coming from inside him. Punching his heart. The door began to shake. He ran to it and grabbed the handle. He could feel it being twisted from the other side. He held it even though he knew it didn't make a difference to hold. It just needed a push. He could feel it lift and pulled downward in response. Three more, right on the other side of the door. More than one person.

Trying to get in. Run to the kitchen, grab a knife. No, run to the bedroom. In the shoebox. He turned, foot placed firmly at the base of the door ready to leap of like a sprinter. Ready to retrieve the shoebox. Ready to retrieve what was in the box and point it at the door. Bolt. He was off the door and into his bedroom in an instant, diving under the bed for the shoebox, instead meeting the large, impossibly bulging eyes of a woman. He froze. The woman stared back at him for a moment, cracked porcelain skin bleeding, eyes black, thin wisps of black hair, before starting to shake, tremor, convulse, then scream, impossibly loud scream, a shriek that deafened him and revealed her bloody mouth, teeth jagged, her jaw becoming wider and wider before falling away completely to the rug, scream still falling out of her. She reached for him. He recoiled in horror and pulled his head out from under the bed, catching his head and then ear as he did, her long broken and bent fingers scratching for his as he pushed away. He fell onto his back, pushing himself away as she, it, crawled, skittered towards him. Three more knocks at the door. Booming, causing him to cringe with each one, only to be replaced with more screams. Screams coming from him as well. Escaping from him. No words. Only terror. He had no plan, only retreat, managing to get to his feet as she reached him, tearing open his leg as he pushed away to the door, her face melting away as she did. In his panic, he had forgotten about the knocking. He pulled on the door. It didn't open. He yanked again. The gurgling scream now right behind him, drowning. He lifted and yanked as it finally came free, falling down the steps, seeing her cracked and bleeding face as he went, her eyes melting now. He hit his head hard on the concrete, numbing himself to the situation momentarily before regaining himself and rolling onto his stomach. She slowed now, reaching out for him from the landing, the skin falling off of her arms now too, her body, soaking what he saw now as a white nightgown, until only raw flesh and then bone remained. She stopped. What remained of her, it, began to crumble. He tried to move. He tried to run but couldn't. Something was keeping him there. It was it. A gust of wind now, sweeping his face and her. She began to blow away, a viciously hot wind sweeping in suddenly, until only ash remained. He began to tremble. *What do you want? Why are you doing this to me?* Saying nothing but knowing it could hear. The dread he felt was mingled. He got to his knees, unable to keep himself upright. It wanted to show him something. Something he didn't want to see. Something he knew inside of him already, briefly, then gone. He tried to crawl away, making it onto her, into her, before collapsing. Please leave me alone. Go. I don't want this. He thought he felt something warm on his face. Something fuzzy. Then nothing.

He woke up sweating. He surveyed his surroundings. He found himself sitting, wedged between the door and the wall. He tried to spring up, instead falling forward onto his hands and knees before getting to his feet and running to the bathroom and vomiting. His stomach was on fire. All that left him was stomach acid and retching sound yet he knelt there, dry heaving, trying. A drop of blood fell in while he felt the heat of it leave his face, and again, until he was able to pull himself to the sink and turn on the tap. The water was warm but he gulped, forming a reservoir with his hands, periodically splashing some on his face, a slight swirl of red at the bottom of the basin. He looked up as the water ran. He must have reopened the cut while vomiting, he thought.

It looked worse than before. He picked at it. Some of the deep red scab fell into the sink and whirled down the drain. His eyes were red, bolts of crimson threatening to consume the whites, the blue, alien on their red background, was glossy and bright. His right eye bluer now then black but ringed sharply with bands of yellow playing around it. He thought of the nightmare the night before. He could remember all of it. It seemed real. I must have slept walked into the corner, slept crawled, he lied to himself. Nothing new. He couldn't remember falling asleep. He sat on the toilet. There was fresh blood on his sock. As he peeled it off, it seemed glued to the bottom of his foot, pulling on the cut painfully between his toes.

6:35am his phone told him. Plenty of time. I'll be early. As he got to the door he thought about putting on his old work shoes but realized his white pair had been ruined by the ash. He put them on instead of the old ones and headed outside. It was very hot and windy today. There had barely been a slight breeze for a few days, save for a few gusts that had stirred the ash horribly, but now the ash had been raining down heavier than before, swirling around the alley, flooding into the garage, dancing about with purpose before piling against the bricks and siding. As he went to the garage, still open, he wondered if that stain was still there under the pile of ash that had blown in overnight. He wondered why the drainage pipe was on the floor behind the truck, though now he thought he had bent it. *Why did I do that? Was I angry?* The truck sputtered to life. As he drove out he could hear the broken top of the bottle roll backwards and hit the tailgate, breaking a little bit more.

He lit a cigarette just as he was leaving the alley. A gust of ash blew through the open window he had opened to ash the cigarette out of. He quickly rolled it up. He ashed on blue plastic that covered the thin grey carpet on the floor. The ash was piling up a bit on the windshield wipers as he drove. When he flicked the switch to turn them on the ash smeared up the windshield in grey streaks. He sprayed some washer fluid but this made his vision worse, ribbons of muddy ash blocking his view out the windshield. He did it again. A little better he thought. Again. Once more and it was clear enough to see out of again clearly. He noted again that there didn't seem to be any other cars or people nearby. He looked up at the windows that he thought the pair had stared out at him before. Nothing. *Fucking weirdos*. A sudden flash in front of him. He pushed on the brake and he hit the steering wheel heavily with his chest. He looked out the passenger window. *Was that a woman*? He tried to lean over to get a better look. He thought he saw her run into the alley to his right. A shout to his left. He looked up to two men running in front of the truck. One stopped and looked at him. Stopped to stare. A snarl. Not a snarl. A low bark. A caught dog. He was off after his friend and the woman. *Are they chasing her?* He tried to jump out of the truck. The handle was stuck. He pushed with force and it popped downward. He jumped from the truck, slipping a bit and ran towards the alley.

Hey! HEY! Stop!

As he entered the alley he saw no one. He kept running. The dumpsters. He ran to the first, looking around the far side, nothing. Second revealed the same thing, as did the third and fourth. The doors! Six in total. He ran too each in the alley, trying to twist every knob and push every lever, until he ended up a few feet from the road. Looking back, he saw the chain link fence at the end of the alley. No way they could make it there in time. *I know I saw something*. Nothing. He got back in the truck. *Should I call the police?* He pressed 911 on the phone but didn't press the green button. *We're they actually chasing her?* He didn't want to be wrong. HE thought for a while before driving off. Looking down the alley as he passed. Nothing again. The wind howled.

As he approached the shop he thought about the story he would tell his boss. His friend. He had been given the job by a man he had met in college, but they had become strained as friends since they had worked together because of his frequent absences, his frequent late arrivals due to those green bottles the night before work. *What will I tell him? I was in the hospital. I was jumped. That will work. That will be fine. He'll see my face.* He passed the building and turned into the parking lot. A few cars he recognized. He was nervous as he approached the door. It was locked. His friend was always there by seven to get things ready for eight. He went to the garage door around back of the lot. It was closed as well.

What the fuck.

He took out his phone. Two texts. From his boss. From his friend. It hadn't rung or vibrated.

All right, don't even bother coming in.

You know what dude, were done. This is last time you're going to fuck me over.

He panicked. *What the fuck.* He reread the texts a few times then he saw it. The clock on the phone. 11:02. *That can't be. Am I hallucinating? It was a fifteen-minute drive. Goddamnit*! He texted back.

Hey, I don't know what's going on dude, I got jumped on the way home last Thursday and ended up in hospital. Somehow, my phone said it wasn't even seven when I left this morning.

He tried calling. Voicemail. He hung up and tried again. Voicemail.

Answer your phone man!

He waited, pacing, his heart racing at the thought of what he would do if he lost this job.

He tried texting him back again. Message send failure. He tried again. Another failure. What in the fuck! He went back to his truck and tried a third time. Failure. He slammed his fist down on the dash. He sat in his truck for a while, rereading the texts and looking back at the time. He decided to visit his parents. He wouldn't tell them about losing his job. Maybe he could convince his friend to rehire him. Maybe.

He sat in front of his parents' house. He didn't know how his dad would react to him being there, on a Monday. He knew that they would question why he wasn't at work on a Monday morning. *What do I say? Do I say he's sick? No. There was something wrong with the equipment? No, the job was cancelled. New project tomorrow. That's fine.* He looked out the grey faded window at his parents' house. Normally a light brick and green home, now tinged with ash. As he approached the door he noticed rust on his father's car that he had never noticed before, a lot of rust looping about the wheel wells and spotting the door. There's no way he'd let that happen he thought. He loves that car. He knocked on the door. Waiting. *What was my excuse? Job cancelled. I guess they didn't pay the deposit. Whatever.* He knocked again. Waiting. What if dad's still pissed? His mom would be awake at this time, no worries. Annoyed he knocked again. He pulled out his phone and texted them both.

Hey guys, you home? I'm out front.

Message Failure. He squeezed the phone in frustration. His mother didn't drive. Where would they go. He walked to the window and looked in, covering his face with his hands forming a canopy as he did. Shock. It looked like his parents living room except not, a room pretending to be in a dream. Ashes had blown in recently and had coated the room in a thin layer. Furniture older somehow, leather cracked, wood pale and bleached. A picture behind the couch hung crookedly, a thick wedge of ash and dust sloped on the bottom ledge of the frame. It looked abandoned. For years. Panic now. He ran back to the door and frantically knocked again, texting them as well and receiving the same message. He tried turning the knob. Locked. 911. He dialled as he ran to the side of the house and reached over the fence and fumbled with the latch. Busy. Again. Through the gate, to the back door. Busy. Again. The drapes were drawn on the sliding glass doors and the handle locked. Nothing. He looked at the phone as it turned black. Dead. Not now. He tried to turn it back on. As he held the button, he calmed himself. *There has to be a reason.* He tried to spy through the individual slats of the drapes but couldn't see anything, only darkness. *There's an explanation.* The phone wouldn't turn on. *There's a reason.* He ran back to his truck. *I'll charge my phone when I get home. There has to be a reason. They're fine.* He sped away.

As he neared his home, he felt calmer. A mound of certainty still crowned lightly with doubt. *They probably left the door open and the ash got in,* he thought. *They'll be safe. They'll... I'll be all right.* Perhaps it wasn't just the house he told himself, something he knew but didn't want to admit to himself. He had lost jobs before, especially in the last two years. He hadn't cared he thought. He'd be alright. Outside of the truck, the wind had picked up again and was funnelling the ash. He had once worked at an industrial wash, cleaning hotel linens. He was done in week. He had worked as a plasma cutter nearly a year before as well. He liked that. He had been fired after falling asleep in his car during his lunch. Passed out. As he thought of these things, the wind and ash howled outside, pushing the truck, an few inches left and a few inches right, rocking it. He reached down to the radio, preferring to leave the music on at a very low volume until now, until now when the ash was worse than he'd seen it and he'd barely seen a person outside in days. He searched, slowly, until he had found what sounded like news. As he looked back at the road, the ash swarmed in front of him, suddenly forming an eyeless snarl trying to consume his path, a lifeless skull of hate, blowing through the vents trying to choke him. He swerved. The truck lead him left. As he covered his face and ducked to escape the ash that was trying to choke him, he pulled the truck right and spun. He screamed, something unintelligible except to him, as he came full circle and the vehicle collided with the high side-walk on his right. He remained hidden until he was sure he had stopped. He slowly peeked over the dash. The ash was slowly raining down onto the windshield and the hood. No longer snarling. He grabbed the sides of his head while he sat up. Breathe deeply. *Just go home. It's been a long day, just go home. You're tired. Just go home*. His truck has stalled during his spin. He tried to start it but stopped, putting his head down on the steering wheel. *Breathe. No, breathe more. A while longer*. He turned the key again; the engine came to life. As he put it back to drive he looked into the left side mirror. Them again. 4 this time. All staring at him. Emotionless from their windows. Emotionless, yet angry somehow. Watching him. His foot began to throb, furiously timing itself with his heartbeat.

Down the alley, he could see that the door was open once again. He punched the steering wheel as he drove. Not panic this time. No fear that someone may be inside.

FUCK!

Just frustration, anger.

As he backed into the garage, he could hear the eaves trough crunch under his left back wheel, and the broken bottle shatter just a little bit more. He didn't care. Leaving through the broken door, he looked down to where the green stain should have been but was now drowned in ash. As he walked up the steps, he could see the ashes had pushed in throughout the day. He entered. He didn't recognize it. The ash sloped in from the doorway into the place, blanketing the living room in a thin sheet of grey. The crevices of his couch had been filled giving the impression that there was only one flat cushion the length of it, and his television had aged throughout the day. The glass he had used the past few nights had partially filled with ash, to the point where it had reached the level of the gold he had been pouring into it, with grey brown smudges spackling the outside, evidence that he had repeatedly lifted and replaced the glass several times since it's last wash with oily, unclean fingers. It looked unused, abandoned for some time. Leaving dark grey impressions, he stomped forward, making his way to his bedroom. There was some ash on his bed and the floor but just a light dusting compared to the living room. He pulled the blanket off of the bed and snapped it in waves to shake off the ash, though most of it settled on the bare mattress, which he swiped at immediately, an attempt to be quick, leaving black streaks on the cream fabric behind. He didn't care. Checking his closet, he saw that the ash hadn't made its way through the cracks in the folding door. He blew at the night table beside his bed, clearing it of ash and began to reach down to the floor to the charger that had slid down sometime during the night but stopped. His mind brought him back to the woman, the thing in his dreams. He backed up. *Not enough.* He backed up more until he was in the doorway and slowly knelt down, tilting his head to the left as he did, until he could see under the bed. Nothing. *Childish.* Nothing but dirt and lint and a shoebox. He wondered about the shoebox briefly but decided not to bring it out from its spot. He thought about how the carpet underneath it must be the cleanest spot in the place. On his hands and knees, he moved the length of the bed to the night table and retrieved the cord, never taking his full attention away from underneath, and plugged in the phone. After a few seconds a battery with a line crossing it appeared on the screen. He thought again about retrieving the box. He stood. He made his way quickly out of the room, imagining an arm reaching out and grabbing him from under the bed as he did. Childish. Into the kitchen. The ash hadn't made its way around the corner. No ash, yet a pile of dishes still and a burnt toaster. A coffee pot that he was sure he hadn't used in two weeks and hadn't cleaned in longer. A newspaper box with an empty garbage bin. A full green bottle on the counter, next to a half full one. A microwave that hadn't been cleaned in four months although he didn't think it had been that long. A flag on the wall and a table with one lazy leg, surrounded by a few chairs and 8 bottles of varying sizes underneath now ready to serve as pallbearers for the table's inevitable demise. He walked to the sink and opened the cupboard above and pulled out a clean glass and turned on the tap. Nothing. What now. He tried the hot tap and water sprayed out, shoving the glass under the tap to collect before it turned too hot. He drank. He had thought before how long it had been since he ate. Now he thought about the last time he had drank water. He dared to fill the glass again, but the steam that followed made him dump it. He tried the other tap again before heading to the bathroom. He turned the hot tap again and filled the glass quickly. As he drank he tilted his head backwards, eyes closed, draining the glass until finished, the tepid liquid soothing, placing the glass on the edge of the sink, opening his eyes. He seized. His pale, bloodless skin had become ringed green with rot stared back at him. His cheeks gaunt and pulled back, dry, exposing his cheekbones. His mouth, lips rotting, open, forced back exposing his black gums, dripping, smiling back at him. His pale grey eyelids lacking moisture, opening to present what was his eyes. His nose, sunken into his face, two black caves. Hair combed neatly to the right. He pushed off the counter, launching himself into the curtain and past into the tub. He groped at his arms at first, each fondling the other, a panicked choke and cough. He grabbed his face. He could see. He grabbed his mouth, his nose. His breathing became heavier, uncontrollable as he rolled his entire self into the tub basin and struggled for air. Desperation. He could see. His nose. His mouth, his lips. He squirmed onto his back. He felt his cheeks. Hot with panic. Grabbing the edge of the bathtub, he tried to push himself up, slipping back in, then succeeding and stared reluctantly back into the mirror. His face was red, his blue eyes staring back at him ringed with red, one with highlights of blue and yellow, mouth an oval, sucking in air desperately, the cut just above his beard worse than before and deep red and black with scab. He screamed, his voice cracking at the end and becoming shrill and painful, and flailed at the mirror connecting with the lower right corner, not shattering but cratering the corner and sending a single fissure shooting across the center. *I'm losing it.* Losing it. He sat on the lid of the toilet and breathed deeply, head in hands. He squeezed his face out of frustration and let a cry out, breaking open his cheek a little more, leaving just a little bit of blood on his palm. After several minutes he stood. Turning towards the fractured mirror, he stared. It was him. Sleepless and damaged. Still him. He reached for the light switch but pulled back and left the light on in the bathroom instead. A night light. He made his way to the kitchen in a state of panic, grabbed the half bottle and went to the living room, opening it on the way. Swallowing, he coughed, swallowed again. As he sat on the couch a puff of ash pushed out revealing the crevices that had been filled in earlier in the day. He placed the bottle on the ash covered table he noticed little marks, little footsteps, five toes each, rat sized, down the center. He stared at them, counted them. Twelve in total. His eyes watered. He breathed deeply, then laughed, brief and low but genuine. He blew towards the table clearing some ash. And again, the footsteps disappearing. Again, his remotes visible. Again, until the table was nearly clear. Taking another drink from the green bottle, he stood. Urrururrururrurrruurrrururr. He could hear his phone from the bedroom. He took another drink, a long one. More water? He thought about going back to the bathroom. He walked out the door instead.

The alley was dimly lit yet somehow, tonight, this didn't bother him. The sky was deeply yellowed. He lit a cigarette and walked, the lighter striking on the first try. He calmed himself, trying to think. *You're tired, a lot has happened in the last few days. You'll be fine*. His mind briefly brought him to when he was younger. When he had asthma attacks that would take his breath and leave him gasping, unable. He hadn't felt that in years. Remnants he thought, his mind drifting to other things. His sister briefly, and his parents, his son. *Hush. I don't want to deal with this right now*. He turned the corner to the right. *Tomorrow*, he thought. *Tomorrow.* He made his way to the doorway. Blues. Closed. The signed looked at him through the glass, taunted him, protected by the pull down steel barrier that was normally tucked away above. Normally a light on at night but nothing tonight. Blackness. He sighed, tossing the butt aside and lighting another cigarette, the lighter lighting again on the first try. It was dark and the ash was falling densely, forming drifts in the street. He turned and walked back towards the alley. This was good. *Just go home. You need sleep. It's been a long day.* He turned the corner to the alley and stopped, wiping his forehead, smearing black the length of it as he did, not knowing he was sweating. He could see his place at the end. He felt dizzy now, it seemed far. He walked. His thoughts soon turned from sleep to the remainder of the bottle on his table. He walked past the garbage, the brick walls and the steel doors that led to the alley once again. Nothing. *Just get home.* He passed the shadowed red dumpster, the bottles and butts and cigarette packs and pill bottle buried under a layer of ash now. Perhaps by a bum as well, he hadn't noticed. Past the open garage door, and the truck and sparse tools and bent eaves. He stumbled over the first step, hopping onto the second and into the door. It opened easily. He stood. *Don't bother with shoes. Leave them on. Couch.* He made his way to the couch and twisted backwards allowing himself to fall, landing awkwardly, safely, on the cushions, ash erupting from either end and settling on the floor. He sat up and groped for the bottle in near dark save for the light coming from the bathroom down the short hall. Urururucuruurrruruuururuur.

He drank. Pause. Breathe, and another gulp. Placing the bottle down, he moved his hand to the table searching for the remote. He studied the buttons with his fingers and pressed what he thought was the power button. Uururrururrruuuuruururrru.

He stood, walking towards his bedroom guided by the bathroom light then the green light of his phone on the night table, grabbing it and pulling it away from the wall rather than separating it from the charger properly. Back to the couch. He sat, picking up the remote as he fell and pressed the power button again. The TV turned on. The rushing sound of static, and the picture that accompanies. He used to imagine it as a million ants racing across the screen, scurrying, trying to get to work and home and baseball as soon as possible. He had imagined that since he was a child. He didn't tonight. Tonight he was exhausted and had a feeling of dread he could not explain, as if his heart knew something he didn't and was beating accordingly, though he would have described it more as restlessness. He pressed the button on the phone. Messages slid into the screen from the right. He stopped. *No. Please No*. He recognized the number. *No.*

Dad, are you there? Dad, I'm cold.

No. His breaths becoming shallow, panicky, as he read. *No*.

Dad, I'm cold. Why?

I'm sorry, he thought. *No, who's doing this to me? Why?* He dropped the phone and stood, backing himself up to the wall on the edge of the couch. *No*! He stared at the phone. One more message. He slid down the couch and grabbed the phone.

Why, Dad?

Dizzy now, he threw his phone towards the wall. It went down the hallway and came to rest against the frame of the bathroom door. After a moment, he ran to it, tears flooding now, searching for her number.

It's dark, Dad.

He found it.

Fuck you, if this is you doing I swear to god.

Why Dad?

Message not sent. He texted his ex-wife again.

Please. Stop.

Message not sent.

He pressed the green button shaped like a telephone. Nothing. Again. Nothing.

He threw the phone back to the floor, just as the television turned to black then back to static. Three separate strikes hammered the door. He stopped, staring at the door. The static turned to black. Three more strikes. One heavy sigh, a breath, then turning his head to the bedroom. He ran, scrambled. Through the doorway, he remembered and fell to his chest several feet from the bed. Nothing. Just a shoebox. Three more strikes. He pushed himself under the narrow gap to the wall and tried to grab the box, pawing, grabbing the lid on the second try. No one there he realized. He pulled it towards himself, out from under the bed and opened. Beads, a book, eight photos, a mechanical piece of steel with a laminated wooden handle, four boxes of bullets. He threw the box on the bed and picked it up. The gun looked loaded. It was heavier than he remembered. He pointed it at the door and slowly walked towards it, noticing his phone face up on the floor as he did. He heard a creak behind him, swinging around and aiming the gun at his bed, expecting to see that thing again. Nothing. Onto his knees. Nothing. Back to the door. What the fuck, he panted to himself.

He noticed the smell now. Wet ashes. Something sour. Something burning.

Why, Dad?

He screamed, pointing the gun towards the phone briefly then back to the door. Silence. For a moment, then three more strikes. The door bulged inward towards him an inch then back out. Breathing. He cocked the pistol now. Outside the window, the sky took a dark red hue, caught fire. He stood still in the middle of the living room now, gun still pointed towards the door. Nothing. Slow. He crept towards the door, turning around once to look into his bedroom again. Slow. Near the door now. He waited for another knock that wouldn't come, trying to will it to happen. He reached for the knob now, building the courage to open. Ready. As he jerked on the door upwards and towards him, gun ready to fire, it burst open, forcing him against the wall, the gun pointing uselessly downwards, dull red light flooding in as well as a deafening sound, a wail. Both there and silent. In an instant he felt crushed, pushed to the ground. He could feel it. That thing. He couldn't see it but it surrounded him, terrified him, trying to show him something he did not want to see. *Please go*. The gun was forced from his hand. He could not speak, nor did it, but he could feel it's hatred, loathing, understand it was evil. Slowly, forcefully, it began to drag him away from the door, towards the kitchen, filling his head with thoughts he didn't understand, visions of horrible things of eaves and fire and stains and death. *No, please stop*. He knew the thing could hear him. *What do you want?* He felt as though he was being pulled from within, from his ribs, the inside of his lungs. He struggled to breathe as he grabbed onto the edge of the wall helplessly. It dragged him around the corner and into the kitchen, holding him up on his knees. There was a shape on the floor he couldn't make out, obscured by darkness, his sight blurred. Distorted. There was a figure above him, standing near the table. The wail seemed to be coming from it but he couldn't make out its features. He could feel the figures pain. The agony it felt filled him while it, the thing holding him in place, torturing him, delighted. Seconds lasting hours as he felt a heartbreak worse than any he had felt before, worse than anything before. The kitchen, glowing red now, the inside of an ember. In an instant, the whole apartment heaved, breathed in, pulsed, red light becoming brighter and the air hot, a furnace, stifling, then darkness as it exhaled, dropping him to the floor. He closed his eyes.

He didn't know how long he laid there, afraid to move in the darkness, curled, frozen, when his mind started racing again. He opened his eyes, straining to see in the darkness that surrounded him. He could make out shapes, a bit of light coming through the window above the table above the green bottles. He crawled, silently, cautious to not make any sound should…*what was that*? The television was on but the program that was coming through was dimly lit he didn't recognize. He made his way along the wall to the living room, springing himself up to the light switches by the door and flicking them on. Still, he surveyed the living room, moving only his eyes. The room was the same. The same as he had it left it in the morning with the addition of the ash. It was still dark outside. He could see his phone near his bedroom door, but waited for something to happen, anything. He was shaking now. Run. He got to the doorway to the bedroom, reaching inside to turn on the light, immediately dropping to his knees to retrieve the phone, pressing the button to reveal it was 12:00am. He saw the woman under his bed briefly he thought, twitched backward and then seeing only the box in the corner. *Was I hallucinating,* he thought. Pushing the phone into his pocket, he remembered the gun and looked back towards the door where he had dropped it to find only ash and carpet. Scrambling on hands and knees, he glanced into his closet before pushing himself under the bed and grabbing the box. He could feel the weight of the pistol as he pulled and lifted the box from under the bed, hitting his head on the bedframe in his haste, running back to the couch, flipping the box open as he did, lid falling to the floor. *I was hallucinating.* Past the book and the photos and the gold. He pulled the gun out of the box and opened the cylinder, revealing the brass and steel contents of its guts. Closing it, he held it in front of him and made his way to the kitchen. There were no figures standing. No masses on the floor. He turned the light on anyway. Back to the door now. It was closed firmly, and staring out of the window, he saw nothing. Nothing but perhaps the homeless man smoking a cigarette in the alley. He walked back to the couch and lit his own, taking a drink out of the bottle. He thought of ergot poisoning. He had watched a documentary about a month ago but now couldn't remember where he had heard about it. *That can cause hallucinations. Maybe I'm just tired.* He held the gun, resting it on his right knee and smoked with his left. No ashtray in sight, he left the butt standing upright in the bit of ash he had missed earlier on the table and picked up the bottle, drinking again then returning it to the table.

When he was a child he had thought his grandparents' house was haunted. He could remember a time with his grandfather when he was young. They had been eating breakfast at the table. It was toast. He couldn't remember where his grandmother or his sister were, but he could remember a very old cartoon on tape featuring a yellow faced rabbit was playing on a tiny black and white TV He could hear a beeping coming from the hallway, a dial tone giving way to the slow, purposeful tones signalling that you had missed your opportunity. He had hung the receiver back onto the pale yellow rotary phone on the wall and returned to his toast and the cartoon. Again, a short time later, he could hear the noise coming from down the hall. He got up to place the phone back on the wall when his grandfather had told him not to bother, and then explained to him the story of the ghost that lived with him. He wasn't a scary ghost he told him, but he likes to play tricks. He'll keep taking the phone off the hook if you keep putting it back. He hadn't reacted to this news except with excitement. He could remember being a little older and playing in an upstairs bedroom with his cousins when the door slowly opened a few inches, creaking loudly as it did, opening with intent too unnatural to be a breeze. One of his cousins slowly crept to the door thinking it was a scheme to scare them, all the others watching him, pulled the door open and yelled 'Grandma!' only to find no one on the other side. That he could remember. At least that's what his memory told him, but time has a way of distorting the truth behind your memories, he thought. *Maybe I'm being haunted.*

Time had gone by. He thought he had fallen asleep for a while but wasn't sure. Dim twilight had just started flooding the sky a dark blue/grey. The gun was still in his hand. He laid it across his lap as he struggled with his pocket, eventually grabbing the gun with his left and standing, pulling the phone out of his pocket. It read 6:30. He had slept. He went to the texts from the night before. None. No messages from his son's number. No texts from anyone saying those things. He placed the phone back down. *I couldn't have been dreaming. That was real. Maybe I actually was hallucinating.* He stood up and went to the bathroom, taking the gun with him as he did, detouring briefly to grab two large glasses from the kitchen.

He held the glasses under the shower head and filled them both as the water heated unusually fast, then grabbed the small one he had left on the counter the day before and filled that one as well, holding the glass so the that the head of the tap was inside of it so as not to burn himself, but burning himself anyway when he pulled the glass away. Instinctively, he turned the cold tap on at the sink but pulled his hand away before burning himself further. The shower had been too hot to enter but he had instead held his towel under the water for a while and rang it out a little bit in the sink before plopping it down. He studied himself in the broken mirror. He was filthy. His hair was matted and powdered grey instead of its usual brown. He had streaks of ash across his face and clothes and but noticed that the ash had almost covered the deep scratch on his cheek perfectly. He must have thrashed about violently the previous night he thought. He thought about his parents again and quickly removed his phone from his pocket.

Hey, I stopped by yesterday and the place was a mess. Let me know if you are okay.

He thought about yesterday as he removed his clothes, revealing pale skin. He could explain his job and his parents' home. He had to have read his phone wrong in the morning. His parents had to have left the door open somehow, letting the ash in. Who knows, maybe they left their phones at home. His mother had been forgetful lately, since his sister had gotten sick again, though he suspected that perhaps she was experiencing something worse, something more permanent than stress induced memory loss. The ash that blew in front of him, he reasoned, simply resembled a face. *You are tired. It's windy. That fuckin fire has been raging for weeks now. You are tired. Maybe you were hallucinating in the mirror. Maybe you were last night as well. Maybe it was a dream after all.* Stress induced nightmares and somnambulism as his doctor had called it when he was a child and he made a point of remembering. Some people get violent when they sleepwalk, have night terrors. As he peeled back the double layer of socks, he cringed. His foot looked like it might be infected he thought. The area around the cut was a deep red now, and redness had groped its way up the top of his foot another inch or so surrounding the wound. He remembered something he should have days ago. He had polysporin in his nightstand drawer he thought. He stood and took the towel out of the sink and placed it on the counter. He stuck his finger into one of the tall glasses. Warm, but not hot. He hung his head over the sink and carefully rained the water onto himself scratching at his hair and scalp as he did. He took the second glass and drank from it before attempting to wash his hair with it again. He scrubbed furiously at his hair with the towel before turning it on the rest of his body, slowly spreading the ash farther before it faded and wiped away entirely. He thought that he should have grabbed clean clothes before coming to the bathroom, or at least a towel, so he didn't have to walk across the carpet wet. He thought that, deeply, he didn't really believe his explanation of the previous day's events. He wanted to.

He had grabbed his shoes on his way to the bedroom and had brought the wet towel with him so as to be able to clean his feet again before putting his shoes on. He left dark teardrops of wet ash behind him as he did, flecking the ground with droplets from his hair as he combed it painfully in an attempt to work out the rest of the dirt and the ash. He didn't care. Not this morning. The more he thought of the night before, of the more he just wanted to get out of the house. He dressed himself and applied a thick layer of the polysporin to his cut before sliding on his socks again, two layers. It burned. He turned to the phone again and searched. It said that the fire that had been raging outside of the city was still far away, 55 miles, and no real way to make the leap to the city from the forest, what was left of it. He went to the kitchen and was struck by the smell of dishes that hadn't been done in a while. He searched the drawers above the cabinets below the countertop. Silverware. One filled with other utensils, spatulas, knives. One with towels. One stuffed with grocery bags. One with odds and ends, batteries, some coins, a small picture hanging kit, a keychain that doubled as a lighter that had long since retired itself, nicotine gum and a small screwdriver set with two of the replaceable ends missing from their home. He thought for a while before walking towards his bedroom, spinning around on his heel, grinding ash as he did, and returning to the kitchen and the drawer that held the forks and spoons and butter knives. Reaching behind the white plastic divider in the drawer, his fingers rested on a loop and he pulled out another set of keys that he couldn't remember his reasoning for stuffing behind there now. He grabbed his cigarettes and lighter off of the table and counted his pockets. 1, 2, 3, 4, 5, and 6. He studied the bottle on the table, thought of the one still in the kitchen. He wanted to drink some. He had a headache from days of sleeplessness and nightmares and hangovers and he knew it would help. No. He returned to the bathroom and drank the third glass of water, filled all three with again with the steaming tap water, afraid they would crack from the heat, and left, slamming the door closed as he did and, unusual for him, locking it.

It was a blizzard. The wind was strong this morning and tunnelled its way through the narrow alley towards him. His garbage from four days previous was still on the ground to the left of the dumpster he noticed. He briefly thought of driving this morning but had changed his mind. For some reason, he did not want to enter the garage. *Besides, the walk will you do you good.* He turned himself against the wind and walked backwards down the cracked pavement to shield himself from the choking ash. Still, the ash swirled around him with the wind changing direction periodically, tides drawing the ash and the heat away from his face before waves charged back towards him, broke, crashed, before flowing away again. An ocean devoid, unsuitable for life to flourish, poisoned and made stale due to garbage and ash, neglect and indifference. He could feel the fine grit between his teeth, grinding it and spit mottled grey into the ash, the impact lost to the storm.

Outside of the alley, the wind calmed a bit. He spun around and began to walk forward. A gust of ash struck him in the face causing him to wince in frustration, before the sidewalk freed itself from the swarm in front of him. He lit a cigarette. 55 miles. He thought that that seemed like a long distance for ash to travel. This much ash, anyway. He wondered whether or not the wind had or would change direction, and if it did whether it would clear the ash away or simply force some that had missed this place before to circle back and strike again. *Kamikaze*. Should have brought sunglasses. This city, this street, it reminded him of the set of an old Spaghetti Western, sepia tone or a photo of a dust bowl farmer stern and committed to his land, almost proud looking, but probably wishing he could leave that place as soon as possible and never look back but afraid of what others would say and think if he did, just like he did. He had watched all the movies growing up he thought. His father probably still kept his VCR all these years too, to hook up to the old Sylvania boob-tube he knew he had in the basement, just so he could watch his Clint Eastwood tapes. He didn't know why that came to mind right now. *I'm the outlaw Josey Wales. Just don't piss down my back and tell me it's raining, world. Now are you gonna pull those pistols or whistle dixie?* As the ash clouded his feet while he walked he threw his finger in a pistol shape, cocked, out in front of him then crossed his left pistol over his arm to aim into the street at his ashy assailant down the alley he had ran through the day before. It was as empty as it had been then. *What happened to her*? As he continued to walk and stare down the alley, he kept his arms crossed, threatening those who were not there, until the alley folded in on itself and out of his view and his attention was drawn to one of the brick apartments and a woman, once again staring at him. No two, another two windows up and…4 to the left. The first appeared to be wearing her nightgown and the second what appeared to be a red dress, no, formal wear, a jacket and blouse. *That's not a nightgown either*. More like an old style of summer dress. Both were old and impossibly wrinkled. Those who watched him. *The Watchers*. He stopped and stared back at them. Fuck the golden girls, if they want to watch me I will too. Both stared at him in the same unemotional way though he realized now that they didn't seem angry like before…sad? He dropped his arms now and faced them directly. *I'm the outlaw Josey Wales. Draw*. His right shooter snapped upward as the hammer fell, directly at the woman in the white dress while, instinctively, the left went up only a fraction later, drawing and firing at the woman in red, both targeted exactly. He kept his arms outstretched for a while. Neither woman reacted. Neither knew that they were shot. Neither knew that they were dead. He lowered his arms. The woman in white finally turned away, closing her grey blinds as she did. The woman in red simply stared. He'd holster these for now. He looked down, hiding his face behind his hand, then his shirt and lit a cigarette. When he looked back up, she was gone too.

It's funny, the things we remember, he thought. He couldn't remember his first kiss. They always show that in the movies. That first. I don't know. Or what you did on your 18th birthday. The last day of high school. The day you won that big game for the team. The day your grandpa died. What he could remember, he thought, were things you hadn't need remember in the first place. The combination to the lock he used throughout grades seven to nine on his green locker. The Ninja Turtle figures his grandmother used to keep for them to play with whenever they stayed the week at their place in the summer. What his ex-wife wore on their first date. A thin purple…blouse he would call it that wrapped around her and ended with a wide collar hanging in front, a black coat that stretch down almost to her knees, faded jeans and what she later called shitkickers. He remembered her eyes. Blue as the corona around the sun at sunset, brilliant and enchanting. He never told her that. He always kept that to himself in case she ever asked him if he remembered, like they do in the movies, but it never came to be, he never got the chance to show her he remembered. He could remember the exact spot he left a trap he and a friend had built on the trail they had ploughed through the trees as children to protect the fort they had built from scraps and old railroad ties. A plastic skateboard with screws drilled through like punji sticks. He briefly forgot where he was going but he was walking the right way.

The ash, the wind, had died down, and for the first time it was thin enough in the air to allow light through that wasn't grey. It was orange, light brown, almost twilight, the sun just as powerful but casting an aura around itself. Hiding itself. The horizon yellowed. *Beautiful in its own way*, he thought. The ash still swirled at his feet but only periodically, inviting him to dance. He obliged. Taking her hand, he spun on his heel and, jumping against the concrete wall of a business he didn't recognize, pushed himself off and landed, legs splayed but upright. He laughed. An actual laugh.

He had been walking, he was sure, but he hadn't known for how long. He knew the streets for many blocks around this particular avenue though. Just a few houses away now. He was afraid of what he might find he thought, but he was sure his parents were fine. As he approached, he saw that the car hadn't moved. It looked more rusted now. Probably ash, he lied to himself, the sun playing itself against the ash. He thought about how his mother would be angry at the fact he was walking across the lawn rather than walking himself over to the path that led to the door. Whatever damage his shoes were going to do though, he thought was already scorched by the ash. At the door. The key still fit perfectly even though he expected otherwise. Still fit. He wondered about his sister. He knocked and, without waiting for a response, turned the key. He breathed deeply, trying to memorize.

He was thirteen in this photo; he could remember that. He and his parents and sister smiled back at him, a white dog with a reddish patch on his head and neck at their feet. They had taken the photo at the cabin his parents used to own. The picture sat crookedly in the frame like it always had, since his father put it there. He jokingly left it like that. He'd make the joke that they had had an OFFuley good time. Nob. The ash weighed heavier on the right. Nobody had been inside the house since the ash had worked its way in. No fresh tracks, except for the ones he was leaving now. He knew they wouldn't like the way it was being ground into the carpet, but it would be evenly stained already he thought, less than two decades after replacing the one with cigarette burns. He walked into the kitchen now. It had less ash on the floor but it was no more disturbed than the ash in the living room. He went to the cupboard and took out a glass. There had been a few dishes left in the sink. Not like them. He turned on the tap. Warm water flowed out, turning to hot quickly. He turned off the tap and took out his phone. 9-1-1. If something had happened to his parents, he had to know. As the phone rang, he wondered if the heat from the fire could cause the…source of the water to heat. He realized he didn't know the source of the water he drank, or how a fire 50 miles away could heat it up so much it came out hot on the other end. He went to the refrigerator but was interrupted before he opened it. The phone stopped ringing, instead letting out three tones in increasingly higher pitch. Frustrated, he dialled again. The phone began to ring just as he heard a loud bang down the hall, someone slamming the door. Cautiously, he looked down the hall, keeping the phone to his ear. Someone was here. He thought about yelling something. He didn't. He walked. Another slam. He could see it had come from his parents' bedroom. Without hesitation, he silently yet angrily walked down the hall, placing the phone back in his pocket as he did, checking inside each of the doors without stopping as he did and pushed the door open with his foot. Nothing. Nothing but ash and an open window allowing it to settle inside, forcing the door to slam and open and slam. He wondered how he hadn't noticed this before when he was in the backyard. He went to the window and closed it, locked it. He thought, *This might make sense.* Maybe his parents were heading out of town. He didn't exactly have a long discussion with his dad the last time. Sometimes when he drank, he forgot things too which might explain why his dad was angry. Maybe he was supposed to go with him and his mother to visit his sister. His sister. Maybe they told him they were heading out of town. He didn't remember sometimes. They had a cabin a few hours away. Sometimes they went with friends. They didn't get good reception out there. They locked the door when they left but must have accidentally left the window open. There was no sign of a break in, anything missing, a footstep on the floor. The bed was made. They didn't leave in a hurry. The only thing different was the ash. The smell he couldn't shake for days now. The heat. The way everything looked older. Slightly decayed. He thought about phoning again but decided that it wouldn't help. He went to the closet and pulled out the vacuum. This was going to take a while.

Hey guys, sorry I missed you. I'm assuming you went out to the cabin and I forgot, or somewhere. Haven't been getting through to you with texts and calls. Anyway, you left your bedroom window open and a bunch of the ash got in. Looked in the window so I tried to clean up a bit. I may have ground ash into the carpet but it looks better. Went and saw Seesaw too. I think they had her in a coma but she looked alright. That's a lie. I'm sorry about last Sunday. Let me know when you guys are back and we can go visit her together. Maybe she'll be awake. I'll keep trying to reach you. Miss you both lots.

Love, your favorite son.

He left the note, written on pink paper, under the wilted flowers in the vase on the table. He looked back as he reached the door. It was a sunny December morning. His parents moved the end table out of the living room weeks before to set up the Christmas tree that he and his sister sat under. It always had too much tinsel and was missing a fake branch, the bare patch always facing the wall. The ornaments he and his sister had made at school. The bird that was missing a leg. His father and mother on the couch, him playing with something that had long since been wiped from his memory. The only present he could remember from that Christmas a blue and black Batman sweater that his parents bought him but that his sister picked out. The carpet faded from under them as they enjoyed their day and turned ashy. He locked the door as he left.

It was cooler now, he thought. There was a slight breeze, not the rushing ashy heat that there was the past few days. It felt nice. He thought he would regret walking as far as he did on the way but he didn't. He had energy for the first time in days. He felt uneasy for a reason he couldn't tell, like something he forgot to do, like when you walk into a room and forget why you are there. He had forgotten to raid his parents' fridge as he had intended but still he didn't feel hungry. He wondered if maybe he was detoxing a bit. *How long does that take? I suppose it could take some time.* He thought of his grandpa. He had fought in the Army in his youth. Seen actual wars. He could remember as a child going through his grandfather's trunk in the basement, the one that held his medals and dress fatigues and glass tubes in hard leather cases and vials and coins blued from age and materials and the gun currently occupying his bed. Every time he visited as a kid, he would go through it and every time he would imagine himself, armed and ready, fighting the other that he was too young to label. It wasn't until he was 14 that he finally figured it out. The vials of morphine. The tubes, needles. The case. He never brought it up. He never went back into the trunk until his grandpa passed, and even then it was only to take the gun, which he had lied about and told his father and family that his grandpa had told him was his should he want it. Huh. His stomach began to hurt. He tried to ignore it. *Morphine seems like a classy thing to be addicted to. You have to be a person of means I guess. Where there is a will, there is a way.* The pull became stronger now, his stomach churning. He stopped and looked to his right. He hadn't been to church since he was a child.

The white cinder block exterior gave way to the wooden eaves and roof and cross. He didn't know why but he tried the door. It was locked, of course. Why would a church be open on a Tuesday. What did he want inside anyway. He stepped back and examined the stained glass. Some saint, some person, standing in the fore. Welcoming arms extended towards him inviting him into his white robed limbs, but a look on his face telling him he may want to stand back, Not a halo. A sun? Something bright behind him in a field of red, blazing.

Can I help you?

He turned. In front of him was an elderly man, white, wearing plaid tucked into khakis above dark red dress shoes. His grey hair sat atop his smile, which he didn't recognize as the first he had seen in days.

I'm sorry, no.

He stuttered and walked around the man, towards the sidewalk.

Are you sure?

He realized he probably looked homeless to the man, covered in ash and grey next to the man's impossibly clean red and blue and beige outfit.

I was walking by, thought maybe it would be open.

Do you want to come in?

I'm not religious.

That's okay, do you want to come in?

He did. He didn't know why.

Okay. If that's okay.

He shook his hand and introduced himself.

He sat in an office. It was nothing like what he had pictured in his mind. Nothing like in the movies. He didn't know what he expected but it wasn't this. It wasn't faux wood panelled walls, lacking Jesus in some way, anyway. It wasn't a newer computer on the desk and a family photo. It wasn't furniture that looked to be out of the '70s around a designer table from some high end store, recently purchased. A glass pen holder with several pens sporting beer brands, or the bookcase behind the desk equally full of history books, philosophy and science fiction. He felt awkward yet very comfortable here. Stable. Sitting on the table was a small golden statue that reminded him of the captain's wheel of a pirate ship. He had seen similar ones before. The man spoke in a soft, purposeful tone.

I got that in a market in Hong Kong about 40 years ago.

People don't question why you have a…Buddhist thing in your office?

It's called a Dhaka. I don't think many people who come in here really know what it is but if they ask I tell them. It's a Hindu symbol too.

And they don't ask why a Reverend has a Hindu wheel in his office?

Well I'm not a Reverend, I'm a Pastor, and yes I've been asked and I explain what it's meaning is. No one seems to care really. You see the spokes in the wheel? Each one of them represents a different virtue or quality someone should possess in order to reach Nirvana. I don't think That's too different from a Christian's idea of reaching heaven or really any other religion.

He arched his eyes and sighed.

I guess not. What do they mean?

Oh, I can't remember them all these days, I probably never could. Love and faith and goodness and …self-control and self-sacrifice…mercy and honesty…hope. Hope. And the others, I mean exactly what one would think you would need to display in order to get to heaven, or achieve nirvana or whatever you believe. Forgiveness, of course, is one.

I'm not… he paused, unsure whether to be blunt and repeat what he had said before… I'm not religious.

You said that. You know, you don't have to be very religious to believe in religion.

That doesn't make sense.

Sure it does. A lot of people are sceptical, a lot of people have always been sceptical. That's why it's called faith. Even if you don't believe in heaven and hell, you can believe in right and wrong, good and evil, or whatever you want to call it. You don't have to believe in god to know the difference.

Maybe, it's not the same thing though. Not hurting someone or…not being a dick to someone, isn't a religion, it's what you're supposed to do.

What do you think the point of religion is, kid? If he were god, why would you want him to want you miserable? Would you believe that he did? I believe that the point of religion itself is to make people happy, and in turn, that will make you happy. Clearly, you were not happy today. What do you think brought you here today?

You let me in.

I know I let you in, but what brought you here?

I don't know.

Sure you do. You tried the door on a Tuesday.

No, I don't know. I had the worst couple of days. Something told me to go in. Maybe I wanted to give a confession. He faked a laugh.

The Pastor didn't laugh.

If you want to do more of a traditional confession through a screen, I'm sorry but this isn't a movie and besides, that's a Catholic thing. A movie Catholic thing at that. I'm not convinced admitting something actually means you're sorry.

I don't know why I'm here, alright? I've been having a rough time, like hallucinations or something, and saw the church. Something told me to come in. Why did you let me in?

Because you look like shit kid, you look like shit but not dangerous. I figured you needed help.

He thought about how he had been walking in the ash and had his black eye and cuts. He wondered how bad it looked.

Are you okay? the Pastor asked.

He didn't answer, just breathed deeply and tried to think of an answer. The priest cut him off.

It's alright kid, you can tell me. I'm a licensed counsellor. You kind of have to be to be a priest.

He thought. *How do I explain?*

What do you mean hallucinations?

He thought back to the hand he felt days ago.

I've been waking up in weird places, falling asleep and having nightmares that I…I don't know how to describe. The freakiest shit and honestly, it hasn't seemed like a dream, it's seemed real every time. Like I'm haunted. He felt odd swearing at a priest

The Pastor waited.

It's like I'm being haunted. Honestly.

The Pastor waited.

It's like I need an exorcism or something. I mean… He wanted to tell him specifics. He chose not to. *I'll keep these to myself.*

Well…again this isn't a Catholic church, kid. I'm a Methodist minister so if it's an exorcism you want, you're better off asking the Pope. Besides these…nightmares, visions, you've been having what else is bothering you?

He thought, briefly, and decided.

I lost my job, my parents hate me, my sister is in the hospital, I'm broke, I'm divorced and my only child died like… He knew the date… a little over a year ago… And now I'm sitting in an office with a Priest asking him to give me an exorcism. I've been better

The Pastor studied him. It would have normally made him uncomfortable but he was calmed by it this time. The Priest spoke.

I can't give you umm…an exorcism, kid. I can listen to your confession, I can do that, but I can't give you ten Hail Mary's or five Our Fathers to make it better.

He waited now, while the Priest thought.

What I can tell you is that one of those spokes is Hope. I hope for you. It's really hope that ties us all together. Hope that things will be better. That they can be better, based on your own actions. Hope that what we do today will affect tomorrow.

He thought the Priest was giving him the standard speech.

And one of the spokes is forgiveness. But I think a lot of folks don't really understand what forgiveness really means.

He didn't respond, just pursed his mouth and waited.

It doesn't just mean forgiving others. Anyone can do that, right? When I was a kid, I fought my best friend over something I can't even remember. I forgave him the next day.

He had done the same.

And some people are…they don't think they've done anything wrong so they don't see a need for it but you…I truly believe that in order to forgive, to actually forgive, you have to see yourself as human and forgive yourself too. That until you forgive yourself, you can't…you can't…you can't forgive others, truly, without understanding the cause. And you can't understand the cause without forgiving yourself. And until then, you might as well be giving a confession to a rock for all the good it will do.

What if I can't? I mean, what if I could never forgive myself for what I did? What then?

You'd have to. Whoever you did things to and whatever you did to them…you have to forgive yourself. You need to find a meaning behind your suffering not sink into it. You may never find peace otherwise. It's easy to lose sight of what is possible but you have to remember that everyone, every life, you will be tested. But if you fight your way through, I honestly believe every single one of us can find the light. Or, you can let the darkness consume you.

They spoke for an hour more. He gave him his card.

He walked, fingering the card in his pocket, folding it and rolling it into a tube and flattening it out again. It felt smooth, plastic, against his fingertips. He folded and refolded the card until it became soft as he walked through the ash. Frayed at the edges. He thought about seeing his sister again, but not today. Tomorrow. Tomorrow he'd be fresh. He'd see his sister. He'd visit his parents. He'd be better. The events of his afternoon already becoming blurred and faint memories. As if they never happened. He turned into the alley, towards his door. It was getting dark. He had left the light on in his place and could see it now. His door was closed. The bum, the homeless guy that was becoming familiar sat in the alley in his regular spot. There was no dog. His white shoes still matched the ones he wore, only more now that the ash had stained them.

Sorry to ask, but can you spare some change? Or a cigarette?

He stopped. He thought. He gave him a few cigarettes and began to walk away but stopped.

Here.

He handed him the change he had in his pocket. The old man smiled. There was indeed a dog under his arm, he could see his face for the first time. It licked the old guy.

Why are you suddenly hanging out in this alley? What I mean is, if you're just asking people for change, you can't be getting much traffic through here.

It's the ash. It's the only place free from the ash. It's been choking me and him.

He nudged the dog.

I suppose there's not a lot of people walking around lately.

Less than you think.

He didn't know what to make of that comment, but he half smiled and nodded anyway, turning, walking away. *I know, old man,* he thought to himself.

As he approached his door, he saw the forms of the bag that had torn open and spread its contents days before, buried in the ash. He had left it there. He didn't know why he wasn't picking it up until now. He picked up the bottles, the broken glass, what he could find, the paper, the empty pill bottles, turning his hands dark with ash. He was tired. Exhausted. He walked up the steps and inside. The place looked awful he thought. He went to work. Exhausted yes, but with a second wind now. He began to clean. He poured water into the glasses in the bathroom as it grew hot, then plugged the sink and allowed the water to fill it up. Dipping a rag into the scalding water, he began to wipe everything down, wipe away the ash. He did the same in the kitchen, immersing the dishes. He went to the hall closet, to the vacuum.

When he was finished, he walked about the place. Dirty yes, but better. He went outside, lit a cigarette but stopped before sitting when he saw him. The rat. He was sitting on his hind legs about fifteen feet away, sniffing the air, one eye darting. Curious. He wasn't disgusted by it this time. As curious about it as it was of him. He went back inside. On the table, left there from days ago, were two pieces of stale moldy bread. He picked them up and went outside. With this ash, he couldn't have eaten well. He sat on the stair while the rat watched him. He broke off a piece and threw it into the ashes. Without hesitation, it bounced over and ate. He threw the other two pieces in front of it. Small pink hands pulling on the slices, nibbling. He smiled. One of the few genuine ones in days. What had disgusted him, choked him days earlier was a reprieve to it, life giving. He could see the old man again in the alley. Red ember of one of the cigarettes burning, given off faint light. He walked inside. He had put the two bottles, one-half full, on the counter beside the refrigerator that he had been unwilling to open this night. He grabbed the lighter of the two and headed back outside. The rat didn't run, stayed and ate. He walked then stood in front of the old man.

Here.

The old man looked at him for a while before reaching out and taking the bottle from him, staring at it like it was something he hadn't held in some time.

Why?

He thought.

I don't know. Maybe I figured you could use it more than me. I don't really want it, to be honest.

He didn't wait for a reply. Walked away. The old man smiled and swigged from the bottle. He hadn't tasted it in a long time. An old man with similar dirty shoes. Again, the rat didn't move from his spot, just looked up at him briefly before going back to his meal. As he went up the steps, the halogen light flickered briefly, went dark, then sparked back to life, though he didn't notice. Inside he drank a glass of warm water, got undressed and went to bed after replacing the box and its contents back in their place. He had no dreams that night, no night terrors no hallucinations. His first restful night's sleep in a week. That thing. That thing that was there and not there at the same time, that had watched him and haunted him would not visit him that night, wouldn't show him what he didn't want to see.

It wanted to.

The sun cut through the grime on the window in bursts and shadows that danced slowly across the wall off of the foot of the bed like constellations in the night sky. He hadn't seen the stars for years, since bringing his wife and son to his parents' cabin. Although he didn't know that. It was the August before he passed away in the night of the car accident. Passed away under the bridge. Drowned. He curled up, hugged himself tightly. He stayed that way until the stars had moved across the wall and faded from his eyes into the darkness of the carpet. Fireflies retreating at dawn. Finally, he relented to the heat. The ash that he had failed to shake free from the blankets clung to the sweat on his body. He sat up and rubbed his face, looking down at his hands. They looked older. He stood, grabbed clothes from his dresser and the floor of the closet. He would do laundry today he thought, go to the laundromat a block away with the missing ceiling tiles and red stencilled letters on the front window introducing an unpronounceable name but cheap soap dispenser. He walked to the bathroom, towards the pre-planned water filled sink and the dirty towel he could use to wipe the streaks off of himself. He closed his eyes as he stumbled along, still groggy from an actual sleep, long enough to misstep and collide his left foot with the edge of the open bathroom door. He cried out as pain instantly shot up his foot and the barely healing wound that circled the webbing of his toes tore open deeply, sponging blood onto the floor as he hobbled into the bathroom and down to the linoleum.

Mother Fucker!

His teeth clenched tightly, grinding against the urge to reach out for his foot before the initial wave had passed, tears forming in his eyes, completely un-numbed like he was the first time. He held his breath, letting out a struggled sigh when he exhaled. He studied the wound through glassy eyes, glaring. Fresh blood was rivering down the top of his foot nearly to the heel. Pain giving way to anger now. The cut itself had torn open. He couldn't tell how deeply but the dark dried scab parted revealing the refreshed wound between.

Goddamnit. God. Damnit.

The words barely escaping his mouth, a whisper, not being said but being pushed out in a hot breeze. He reached and opened the drawer. Pulling out the only clean rag. He had left the tube in his bedroom. Pushing himself up, using the tub and the toilet, he laid the rag on the floor and stood on it, slowly turning red while soaking. He looked in the mirror. Pale. The bruise under his eye was more yellowed now. The cut on his cheek black. Darkness under his eyes, his cheeks and temples lined with burst blood vessels. He began to cough. He snatched and drank the glass of water he had left on the counter the night before, quickly, desperately before the coughing passed. Pulling the towel off of the curtain rod, he dabbed it into the sink.

He stood outside. The wind had picked up today. He stared into the garage. Months before he had gotten a flat tire while leaving work and failed to get it repaired or buy a new one. Now, as he looked inside, he could see he wouldn't be driving that day. The front right tire was deflated. He imagined that it was because of the swerve he had made a few days before. Defeat. He thought about staying home, not going to see his sister. He briefly thought about picking up the bent piece of eaves trough that he just now noticed was actually two pieces bent together and punting it through a window. That thought had almost won. His foot throbbed underneath the layers of cloth and sock. He thought about the last bottle on his counter. He lit a cigarette and began to walk down the alley, the wind tunnel. He saw the empty green bottle leaning against the brick wall as he passed, half buried in ash already, having accomplished its purpose, now tossed aside. As he crossed into the street he entered a ghost town, save for the eyes of those who watched he was too preoccupied to notice, staring at him from the apartment windows. He felt uneasy. A pain in his chest pushed in as if he had just been running and then subsided. He spit and dug ash out of his nose and rubbed his fingers together. For some reason, he thought of the green stain under the ash and the eaves kicked into the back of the garage.

It was after her first two weeks of university that she phoned home crying late one night. She had told him before she left that he was nervous about being alone, about knowing no one and living with strangers. She had a problem with anxiety, something that always caused her to shy away from people, even their parents at times, but never him. He drove nearly a quarter way across the country that night only stopping at a grocery store sometime in the morning. He never told her he was coming, just showed up at the university, got her room number from the front desk and surprised her at her door. He made her favorite breakfast, their grandmother's sweet barbecue sausages and French toast, even invited her roommate's out to eat with them. He could tell that after two weeks his sister still didn't really know these two other girls. It was a quiet, simple conversation, one-word answers, despite his efforts to summon longer ones. That night, he got them all to go out bar hopping with him, on 'the strip'. Once they've had a few drinks, they'll get louder. They did. On the walk home, there was laughter and he thought he could remember giving one of the roommates a piggyback ride when she got too tired to walk. He woke up on the couch in the morning to his sister and one of the others eating leftovers and giggling about the professor and complaining about at a class they didn't know they shared. He pretended to sleep a little while longer. To give her time. Those two remained friends as far as he knew, though he hadn't asked her about the old roommate for a while. He wondered about her. When he left that afternoon, his sister told him she loved him, hugged him. He could remember her smile. He could remember winking at her. Their little symbol when they both knew what was up. She winked back.

He stopped at the store on his way. The green metal siding advertised their hours and the great deals you'd get for points you'd receive for buying their gas but was betrayed by the rust that was consuming the edges of each strip of tin and the grime that had built up on the window. He pulled on the first door but it was still locked, the other opened. He entered and walked to the newspaper rack. There were government budget cuts to education, there were 12 dead in Mexico border violence, there was a deadly crash on the highway. He scanned the stories that bordered the headlines. A sport star disgraced, a dog saves owner's life, what the warnings signs are to tell if his child is a drug user. Nothing about the fire. He felt dizzy and his eyes watered a little. He rubbed, turning towards the cashier, her face melting into a horrible grimace as she oozed towards him, mouth ready, wide, dripping black and clawing out towards him. He twitched, startled backward into the newspaper rack. He grabbed at his shirt collar and lifted the inside to his eyes, rubbing away the blur for a second and looking back up, ready. The cashier looked at him in a way that told him he may have appeared to her like a lunatic.

Sorry.

She said nothing. Stared. He bought his cigarettes and again chose the wrong door before exiting. He lit a cigarette as he walked past one of the signs that told him not to paste on all four pumps. He imagined it exploding.

Pppkkkkooowwwwwwwwhhhh

The uneasiness never left him. It didn't grow stronger, just more sickly as it moved from his chest to his stomach. He had been preoccupied until now but his foot was throbbing again. He was still blocks away. He could feel the warmth and stickiness of fresh, coagulating blood building up in his sock, the fibres of the clothe becoming sharper with each step, pushing into the wound. The ash, the wind, seemed no better, no worse, yet different. The sky was yellowish grey. Grey clouds swam above him, torrents and whirlpools. It was beautiful he thought, yet absolutely terrifying. Otherworldly. *The methane skies of Venus.* The same feeling of dread started to come over him. He lit a cigarette and began to walk faster. For a very short time. The pain in his foot made him switch to walking on his heel now. Hobble. He could see the parking lot in front of the hospital. A car, old and rusted, first one he'd seen on the road in days blew past him, sending a wave of ash covering him like a splash after a storm. The car swerved left down another street, screeching the corner at speed. He crossed the road into the parking lot still hobbling, though now slowing. He calmed now and started to feel foolish. The parking lot was nearly bare. Maybe these people, these sick and dying, had relatives as bad as him. The hospital walls were grey with ash, windows dark. He made his way up the wheelchair ramp, rather than the stairs, up to the pale blue doors that were the main entrance. He stood at the door clutching the rounded metal handle.

A greying man pushed his way down the corridor. He seemed lost, clutching the metal rod that suspended what seemed to be an empty IV drip whose tube was filled with a yellow liquid, bile, and lead up his forearm and disappeared under his sleeve. The receptionist was missing again, though she had left stacks of files and papers on the front desk as well as a filing cabinet open. He rounded the corner towards the corridor he needed. The floor was colour coded with lines and arrows to direct you to your destination though they had faded terribly since he first came here. Since she first got sick and started to come in for her treatments. He opened the steel door to the stairwell. He regretted not taking the elevator, as it was impossible not to use his toes to climb the steps upwards. His footsteps echoed. Into another corridor. He hoped she would be awake this time, responsive. He hoped to see her eyes again. Give her a wink. He stood outside her door for a moment before turning the knob and entering. Fresh folded white linens sat upon the naked bed. The flowers, the picture frames, the stuff she requested be brought from her home, the CD player she still kept for years because she refused to buy an mp3 player, gone. The machines that had been monitoring her, feeding her, medicating her, all gone. The heavy curtains closed once again. He stared around the freshly sanitized room, knowing what it meant in the back of his mind but refusing to let himself say the words internally. He began to shake, his eyes and mouth wide. He almost collapsed. The weight of a thousand memories came flooding over him, threatening to collapse him. A nurse suddenly entered, slamming the door, paying him no attention, only the bed. She began to shake out the sheets, the light blue blanket on top, make the bed. He stared at her. He couldn't see her face but her hair was a tangle of grey and black.

Excuse me?

She kept making the bed.

Hey, he said softly, excuse me nurse?

She turned to him. She had almost black eyes that sat, bursting, on her unnaturally pale, thickly makeuped face. Thin red lips torqued into a smile framing corroded teeth. Her light blue scrubs stained in the front with red and burgundy and maroon. She said nothing, only smiled.

Where is she?

Where is who, my dear? Her smile never leaving while she spoke.

What do you mean where is who? Where the fuck is my sister? The woman who's been in this room for months? Where is she?

She stared back at him, her head seemed to wobble a little as she continued her forceful smile back at him. She said nothing, only blinked.

Tears were forming now, hotly making a path down his cheeks.

What is wrong with you? Where is my sister?

My child is dead. A familiar voice from the doorway as the nurse slowly swivelled and turned, eyes forward as she did. His father stood in the doorway. Wrecked, he shuffled into the doorway and let himself fall into one of the armchairs in the corner. He wore an old t-shirt he would normally only wear in his garage or in the garden and jeans that has long since been presentable. His face was grey and red from grief, his eyes black and red from sleeplessness. He slowly looked up at his son, tears welling in his eyes. He looked back at his father as he backed himself against the wall and slowly slid down the wall onto the floor, chest heaving, trying not to be overcome but unable to stop the tears. He began to sob.

When?

Last night.

He thought of his decision to not go over there yesterday afternoon. His stomach ached now and he closed his eyes tightly until he could see nothing but darkness. He opened them and looked at his father who had his head in his hands now, body moving in rhythm with each heavy, silent sob.

Dad. I'm sorry, he said, but received no reply. He stood up.

Where's Mom? Where were you two the past couple days I went to your place. Still his father did not look up, only sobbed. He went to him and stood in front, putting his hand on his father's shoulder. Eventually, his father stood as well and embraced him. Shaking. He could remember what it was like for him and now his father's grief threatened to overcome him as well. He could feel it radiating off of him. His father gripped him tighter now and stopped shaking. They hadn't been close in a while. He wished this could last a while.

It should have been you, he whispered, hugging him tighter now. He thought he had misheard. He kept hugging back.

It should have been you, his father said again, digging his fingers into his son's back before shoving him backward towards the wall.

Look what you've done! His father growled at him, pointing towards the bed, this is your fault!

Dad, what the fuck! he cried, looking towards the bed. He stopped. He couldn't breathe. His eyes wide and glossed. This felt familiar. A nightmare he had had before many times. The smiling nurse, the sheets and blanket, gone. A boy. Motionless. Leg casted and raised. Stomach heavily bandaged over dozens of stitches and pale bloodless skin. Arms scraped raw, stabbed with synthetic veins, finger attached to a clip. His neck surrounded by a white plastic brace. And his face. Tube running into his toothless mouth, above a broken jaw. His crushed nose covered and protected. His eyes black. His head, shaved, broken, bandaged, with screws protruding and orbited by a steel halo. Machines surrounding him. After it all, unthinking and unwakeable from inhaling cold water. He became mad at the sight of his son. He ran over to the dying boy, screaming. This is how he had left, years ago. He cried uncontrollably, held his son, careful not to move him but squeezing. He turned his head and put his ear to the boy's chest, closed his eyes, listening for a heartbeat. He stayed there, feeling the boy's lungs being inflated and deflated on command, but unable to stifle his howls long enough to sense a beat. He looked up to the boy's face. It was still. Except for the eyes, they twitched with what he thought were dreams. He had hoped that meant that somewhere, deep inside, that his son wasn't gone, that his mind wasn't traumatized. The continued, rapidly moving, bouncing, until they flashed opened. Slowly, they scanned over to meet his.

Monkey? he choked.

His son said nothing. Only stared back at him through familiar eyes. As his tears fell on the boy, they began to sink and puff into his frame like rain into ash. He felt his son's ribs start to weaken and snap. He stood up as the boy's face sank into the cot, his stomach, his arms and legs quickly greying, crumbling, beginning to blow away, becoming dust, until all that resisted were his eyes, still staring at him, accusing him, until they too turned to dust. He screamed.

NOO, NOOO, he screamed, over and again, unable to make sense of what was happening until his father grabbed him from behind and turned him. His face was distorted, pocked with black pits burned deep into him.

This is YOUR FAULT! His father's words vibrating inside him. He pushed him up against the wall now, his fingers, again, digging into him, gouging his shoulders.

YOUR FAauullllaaaaa. His words falling apart just as his face was. Terrified, he turned his face away. He could feel the hot breath on his face, the taste of sulphur in his mouth as he screamed. He twisted, pushed, trying to get away, throwing his father, this thing and himself onto the floor. It howled as it collapsed into the floor, shattering like a glass against the linoleum, pieces of itself ricocheting around the room until the shards turned to dust leaving only the echo of the howl that reverberated inside his head, growing louder, unbearable. He pushed himself back against the wall, covering himself with his arms. The neon lights toyed with him before burning out, leaving him alone in the darkness of the room.

His heart was racing, trying to escape. He felt his way along the hospital floor to the doorframe. He lit his lighter as he peered around the corner but it only blinded him more and he quickly let go of the trigger. He didn't think of staying in this room only escape. He felt his way across the hallway, terrified of what was in the darkness, until he felt the ribbed baseboard on the opposite wall. Slowly, he groped his way along, each shuffle, each baby step a moment of uncertainty followed by relief as he found solid ground once again. He counted the doors as he crept, trying to decide how far along the hall he was, which door was his. This one. Did the stairwell have a knob or a handle? He pulled down on the handle and the door creaked open. He lit his lighter again. A woman, bent into the corner under the hospital bed, eyes stitched shut yet sensing his presence growled and lunged at him like a dog baring her teeth. He pulled back on the handle to close the door dropping his lighter in the room as he did. Elbows unsteady, he crawled on to the next door, the will to escape overriding the will to give up. He felt a knob. Quietly, he turned it. Still no lights in this room. His hands led him across the floor, guided him until he came to what felt like a metallic rise in the floor. Relief as he gripped the first step. He began to make his way down, holding each with purpose until his palm ground into something slick and wet causing him to fall forward onto his face and tumble and slide down the rest of the steps, hitting the door below hard.

He stayed there awhile, heaped into the corner next to the door. His ribs ached, and he could tell he was bleeding from somewhere on his face, but where exactly he did not know. His eyes tried to adjust to the darkness but no light could penetrate into the stairwell. *Nothing is here* he thought. *Nothing is in here now trying to get here. You're alone. Now get out.* He stood, painfully, palming the wall until he found the door and the knob. Deep breaths. He gritted his teeth and turned the knob slowly to not alert whatever was on the other side. He pulled and attempted to slide into the hall but, ill-timed, caught his shoe on the door and almost fell, his left hand propping himself up from the floor. Something was wrong. There was a faint glow of light coming from an unknown source revealing shapes and objects but he couldn't make out what they were. He gripped the floor. Carpet. *Carpet?* He widened his eyes in an attempt to see better. He stood. There was a light switch next to the door but it didn't work. He thought he knew where he was. *No.* He could see the outline of another door and scanned the floor in front of it to check for obstacles but could not see any. *Move.* He walked to the door fast, with purpose, grabbing the knob, twisting, lifting upwards and pulling it open. A blast of light and heat burst through his front door, stinging his eyes. He pulled back and scanned his living room. There was ashes blanketing the room worse than before. The smell of something rotting and sulphur was intense. He tried to make sense of things.

Uurrurururururrurururururruurrr

Don't move. Stay. Don't move. They can't get you if you don't move. Just stay here.

Urrururururrruururuurururrruuu

He watched his phone. It was sitting on the end table by the couch, slowly vibrating its way across the glass though he couldn't remember leaving it there. He couldn't remember leaving it anywhere. Today couldn't have been a dream. *I'm losing it,* he thought, *I need help. I need help.* He waited. Hunched by the door, he made sure to keep an eye on his bedroom. *Had I really never left this morning?*

Ururuururrruruuururuururururu

The phone made its way to the edge and fell, landing softly on the carpet in a puff of ash. He watched it from across the room, afraid to move from his spot next to the open door. The heat pouring through was intense, worse than it had been in the past week. His ribs hurt from the fall he wasn't sure happened. He lifted his shirt and saw the red marks on his side. He thought and began to crawl, silently. He could see through the bedroom door under his bed to the shoebox. He kept his attention on the box, and began to crawl towards it, stalk it. *Nothing can get me if I don't look away*. Through the bedroom door, he crawled. Onto his belly now, he squirmed under the bed and slowly pulled the box out as he wiggled his way out ahead of it. He backed his way out of the room, back into the corner by the open door, grinding the ash into his pants and the carpet in parallel paths. Sitting on the floor, he pulled the pistol out of the box and opened the cylinder. It was empty. He felt around the shoebox until he found one of the boxes of bullets. He slid them into the chambers and put the rest of the box in his pocket. He slid the shoebox behind the door and stood up. He pointed the gun at the phone and walked towards it but caught himself and lowered it, finger on the trigger. He moved it to his left hand and picked up the phone and turned, keeping his back to the wall. He held the phone, staring at the blank, dark screen, thumb on the button that would light it up but unable to press it.

Uurrururrrururrrururrrururur

It vibrated in his hand and lit up. He shook as he read it.

Why did you leave me in the hospital dad? This is your fault.

Anger now. Hate for whoever was doing this to him, worse than he'd ever felt it before. He heard a crack, not realizing he had squeezed the phone until the screen shattered in his hand. He pitched the phone against the wall and watched as it broke apart, putting a long dent in the drywall, switching the gun to his right hand and firing two shots at the phone, hitting a piece once. He kept the gun raised at nothing for a while, unsure of what he was aiming at. He looked towards the open door. Heat poured in, heat and ash and light. A crash howled in the distance the echoed through him. He walked to the doorway, calmly, and stood on the concrete landing, staring out into the alley.

The sky was a pale red, a sea, darkly swarming with whirlpools of dust and ash, blocking out the sun, casting shadow only broken by flashes of light flaring through the clouds followed by thunder. He saw it. Something, a shadow, darker than the rest, slowly moving to the center of the alley from behind the brick buildings that lined the street ahead of him. He raised the pistol towards it as he backed into the house, slamming the door behind him and heading to the window. A tightness came over his chest, making it difficult to breath. The shadow kept coming towards him, stopping near the door, watching him without eyes, speaking to him, threatening him without lungs, without breath. This thing, this evil thing, wanted to harm him, but couldn't somehow, something was stopping it. A piercing scream shattered the silence. The thing laughed. The scream was coming from the kitchen he thought. He turned and backed into the corner, away from the window. He couldn't see the shadow anymore but he could feel it as he kept his eyes on the opening that led to the kitchen, raising his gun to it. He leaned around to look out the window though he couldn't see the thing anymore. He jumped and spun, pointing the pistol out of the window but saw nothing but ash and red and someone running on the street past the alley. He stepped forward towards the entrance to the kitchen, keeping the gun pointed but looking out of the window. Two more men ran by the gap in the alley followed by what looked like a woman only bigger and faster than a person should be capable of. He stepped again towards the kitchen as the scream turned into a wail. He could feel it now, the shadow, grasping him inside his chest, his stomach. He was close now. He didn't fight it now. Just crept to where it wanted him. He got to the wall now, feeling his hand drag against the bubbled and brailed paint. He grasped the edge. The shadow pushed him forward. Deep breath. *Go*. He swung the pistol into the kitchen ahead of him. A woman stood in his kitchen with her back to him, shrieking and crying.

Turn around.

She didn't.

Turn around now, I'll shoot.

His voice cracked as he spoke. Again, she didn't. He raised the pistol and pointed it at the crying woman's back and crept, momentarily contemplating hitting the woman with the gun, around the ledge and discovered what she was wailing over. It appeared to be a man, blurry though recognizable as a person. His skin appeared grey against the rug though he couldn't make out features. The pressure grew inside him now, it wanted him to see. He stepped towards the side of the woman, pistol still raised though more casual now, to try to see her face. The gun dropped to his waist. Her grey hair was set back into a ponytail, red glasses filling up with fog as her breath fled upwards from hands softened with age that were cupped over her mouth as she tried to calm herself unsuccessfully, lines on her face from laughter and cries, both of which he had caused. Yellow loafers under jeans under a ruffled green sweater, the one he had bought her years ago for mother's day.

Mom? He began to cry as he looked down at the mass on his floor, oddly familiar but still unable to see its features.

Mom? Look at me.

She did not. Ignoring him, she now knelt and placed her hand on the person, the mass on the floor. She shook the leg and wailed again as she did. Whatever it was, it was stiff and cold. He could feel it as well as she could in that moment. An intense feeling of sadness and loss that he had felt only once before in his life but knew more intimately than any other feeling he had ever experienced. He trembled as she stood again, crying, staring at her eyes that had swollen and reddened and glazed with tears. He watched as she turned towards him, hoping for her to stop and talk to him, to hear her voice, but instead watching her move towards the doorway and slowly walk into the living room, hunched and defeated as she went.

Mom, he said once again, knowing she couldn't hear him but not understanding what was happening in the moment. He followed her ghost into the living room but she was no longer there as he entered after her. His door was open. He walked back into the kitchen. The form on the floor was gone, probably never there he thought, just an apparition he thought. He picked up the bottle that sat on the counter, knowing its contents may make him feel better for the moment and returned to the living room. He sat, placing the bottle on the ashy table with his left hand while holding the pistol with his right before returning the bottle to the kitchen. He tried to make sense of things. *They aren't real. They can't be real.*

He stared at a patch of rug, his mind straining. He imagined placing the gun to his temple, then did that. The steel felt cold. He imagined pulling the trigger. He sat imagining. *Crazy people don't know they are crazy*, he thought.

A large chunk of concrete burst through his window into the back of his television, sending shards of glass across the room and waking him from sleeplessness. He jumped to his feet, pulling the pistol from his temple and aiming it at the window. It was dark now. He could hear people yelling in the street. Someone ran away from him down the alley though the shadows obscured his vision. He burst through the door, angry, chasing the culprit down the alley until he lost sight of him when he turned down the street. He slowed then. Holding the gun with both hands, pointing it ahead at the bricks where he last say the brick thrower, he crouched and stepped forward carefully, not thinking about the day's events or the weeks.

It won't help.

He spun and pointed the gun to his right, ready to shoot, until he noticed it was the homeless man. Lower the gun. A loud crash of thunder again followed by a flash. Ash swirled into his eye. He rubbed as he spoke.

Did you see who did that? The rock through my window?

It won't help.

What won't help?

Trying to chase him. Getting him back. It won't help.

He stared at the old man.

What are you talking about? Some fucker just put a rock through my fucking window!

He laughed. Yeah I saw that. But you chasing him won't help. Being angry won't help.

More screaming, yelling from the street now.

What is going on out there?

Don't know. Don't care frankly.

Don't care? It sounds like a goddamn…fucking…riot.

Go home. All I know is when the world goes to shit don't add to the pile.

What?

Whatever is going on out there, it's not going to help you to join in.

He stared at the old man. A light beside one of the back doors to the long brick buildings lit up for the first time since he could remember. He pointed his gun at the door, waiting for someone to exit, though he quickly thought better and lowered the gun. He looked back at the old man. This was the clearest he had ever seen him, though not completely without shadow. His shirt and vest and coat still in the order he first saw them in but his greying beard and shaggy hair were concealing something more familiar now. For a moment, he thought he knew him. Something about his eyes. Something about his voice. *I swear I know you.* He opened his mouth to say something, what he wasn't sure yet, when the ground tremored preceded by a loud crash. Fire tongued from two of the windows of the apartment building across the street from the alley, chased by black smoke.

He ran towards the building. As he reached the street, he saw the body. An older man, about 60, lying on the sidewalk under one of the windows. He heaved. Nothing to vomit. His charred body ended at his hips, the rest of him torn away, gone, his insides spilled off the sidewalk into the street. Ropes of deep red and purple and black. Gory streamers lying in a pool of blood dampened ash. Screaming. He heard a woman screaming from inside the building. He didn't hear his own voice screaming. He stuffed the pistol into his waistband and looked around the street expecting police. Nothing. No sirens, no lights. Another bang. He could see Blues in the distance, the brick surrounding the front cage began to crumble into red and grey dust into the street. A man ran towards the broken building and threw a brick through the window above the ledge he had sat on less than a week before, and jumped into the building. Screaming again, coming through the open doorway. He stared at the opening, scared. Hesitating. The events of the past few days had made him wary but angry. He ran through the doorway. Smoke filled the hallway and stairway neighbouring it. The screaming was coming from above. He ran up the steps, tripping on the 5th but regaining himself and continuing. In the second floor hallway, the air was hazy. The screaming continued from above. Third floor. *On your left. Next door.* He felt the handle. It was warm but not hot. He braced himself. Hiding behind the wall that was hiding behind its own yellowed wallpaper. He twisted and pushed, cowering away from the doorway. No flames but the screaming grew louder. He entered the apartment. He began to cough as smoke filled him. He crouched and crawled now, the smoke swimming above him, through the kitchen in the living room. She was there. A woman in a white dress, ashed grey now, lying on the floor near the front window. He hurried on the carpet, between the brown and green and beige couch and chair, to her. She was bleeding. Stomach. Blood pulsed out of her abdomen. He placed both hands and pressed like he had saw in the movies. Her face was pale and she looked directly into his eyes, terrified.

Where am I?

Her voice warbled as he noticed a pond of blood behind her head.

I'm scared.

I'm going to get help, he promised. He backed up on his bum into the kitchen cabinets, knowing then that he didn't have his phone. He stood. The smoke choked his eyes. He felt along the walls trying to find the exit. A piece of plastic. An old Bakelite telephone on the wall. He pulled it free from the drywall and dropped to his knees looking at it for a moment. It was ancient, the curled cord running to the wall above him to a patch of unpainted wall and a small plastic pad from where the cord snaked. He stood again, left hand trying to think of numbers, receiver tucked between his cheek and shoulder, right on the counter, searching through the smoke to see numbers. Stabbing pain. He tried to twist to his right but he couldn't. A long polished shard of steel with a cheap black plastic handle through his hand, and into the yellow sequined counter top. He looked up. A man. Not a man. *A thing*. Smiling at him. Smiling through shattered teeth, daring him. He dropped to the floor but his hand was stabbed through, pinned, tearing the muscles and tendons. Its red face licked its lips with a forked tongue and turned towards the woman. He pulled up his hand stopping at the handle. It licked again and turned its head towards the woman. It wore nothing. Its crooked body sparsely covered in black hair. Watching, he grabbed the knife and pulled, trying to get it out in a panic. It crouched towards her, savouring. She looked at him, locking eyes, begging him to help. It opened its mouth. Blackness inside and dripping onto the floor like tar. He looked at the blade, trying to keep his hand straight as he slowly slid his hand back down, the blade causing a suction inside his hand as he pushed. It wanted her neck. It looked at him them back to her. She looked, kept her eyes locked on him, begging him. It snapped. Blood sprayed as it began to chew on her neck, her throat and veins. He jerked upwards again but the blade was too deep. Wait. The pistol. He reached behind him, feeling for the gun, touching the steel but not being able to grasp. He pushed his hip against the counter until he could reach it, whipping it towards the living room. The thing gnawed, holding pieces of her in its claws, eating them. He pointed the pistol at it then towards the knife. He aimed at the blade and pulled the little metal moon, the handle of the knife a baton twirling into the smoke. He pulled up and freed his hand, looking back at the living room. She was clearly dead now, her head nearly freed from the rest of her. He fired three shots at it, appearing to strike it once in the head. It looked at him, held her arm, took another bite and smiled. He began to run, choking on smoke as he fled.

Blood dripped from him but he didn't notice. *Get home.* He ran down the stairs, swinging himself by the railing around the corners. Second floor. A small girl standing in the smoke in a bloodied nightgown staring at him, black oozing from her mouth. *No. Keep running. It wants you to stop.* Away from the building, no longer caring about the woman, forgetting her, ashes following him as he ran. Almost there. His hand was on fire. Smoke in his doorway. An explosion ripped the air behind him though he didn't turn around. The old man, the bum, was no longer there, his area ashed in already. Never was. More fire coming from the building on his right and a tremor growing beneath him threatening to topple him. He saw it and stumbled before falling to his knees and tumbling, as quick to rise as he was to fall. A shadow, a mass of darkness in his doorway, begging him to come to him. He ran towards it. Gun pointed. I'm ready. No I'm not. He faltered, dodging into the garage and fumbling in his pocket for his keys. 1, 2, 3, 4…he found them and jumped in. Starting the engine with his slick, bloodied hand he looked up through the windshield. Countryside. A dark highway.

He recognized the blue gauges informing him and felt the fake leather handle on the gear shift, hand groping it past a long grey flannel shirt. The cut through his hand had disappeared. He watched himself, living again that day. Please stop. It was as if he could see his eyes and use them to see at the same time. Not this day. Not again.

Dad? His son asked. He looked at his son. His blonde hair flat from sleep. His tired blue eyes looking up at him, just waking up after hours of dreams that came to an end. He looked back towards the highway. The white lines smudging into a continuous chipped and blurry streak. He looked at his hands gripping the steering wheel as he drove. The radio was on but he didn't recognize the song. *Pull over you idiot. Not again.* The alcohol on his breath momentarily stung his eyes as he drove.

Almost home, bud.

They weren't. He knew that. Only twenty minutes prior he was picking his son up from baseball. Now he had only minutes to think, minutes to have memories and thoughts and ideas. Hopes and dreams. Maybe a day to live. *Look at him fucker!* He placed his hand on the boy's knee and squeezed but never looked over. A truck up ahead. A truck he would have noticed had he been sober. It had broken a timing chain earlier in the day and had been left where it died. He could see it fast approaching. His eyes grew heavy and he blinked with purpose. *Please, I don't want to see this.* He had had no memory of the accident only saw pictures, only watched the boy die in a hospital bed. But he knew what happened. The vehicle began to slowly drift towards the shoulder of the road. He couldn't fight it. He yawned, causing his eyes to water right by the truck now. He rubbed his eyes, causing him to pull the vehicle even more onto the shoulder. Rumble strips on the side of the road catching his attention. He opened them up just in time to see the accident. His car collided with the truck forcing both into the guardrail. The sound of crunching metal and broken glass filled the void around him. His son, not wearing a seatbelt, launched forward. His head hit the windshield, not going through but punching the safety glass out an inch before he collapsed onto the seat. His neck broken in two places. The truck caught a gap in the guardrail that led to a truck stop causing it to abruptly stop and flipping the car over end onto the roof before sparking flipping into a small creek, forcing it to a stop on the rocky bed. A green bottle popped up from the back seat and struck him in the back of the head. The steering wheel in front of him had been bent towards the dash from his forehead. His face swelled and he could feel the warmth of blood in his hair. His son's legs were protruding out from behind him, the rest of him crumpled and bleeding from his eyes and ears and nose. Light from the truck stop shimmered silver across the rivers of blood that flowed. He tried to pull the boy back into his arms but didn't have the strength. He pulled at the seat belt that had held him in place, dropping him awkwardly onto his neck. He could smell oil. Oil and sulphur, he thought. He shuffled towards the boy, pushing himself forward and sliding through the broken glass. He closed his eyes again.

He didn't know where he was now. Nowhere. Inside his own mind, his own memories all he could see now, lost in the darkness. Not awake but not asleep, more a dream than anything, playing the movie of what he had been told. They had laid there, undiscovered, until the morning. A dairy farmer with mud covered boots and overalls had discovered them during that small period between total darkness and sunrise. He had been lucid, he had been told, walking around, smoking until the paramedics had arrived, muttering nonsense, occasionally shouting for his son. He had broken his arm and suffered a concussion. His son was much worse. In addition to his neck, he had been bleeding inside his skull for the past eight hours. Mostly, he had slumped, his arm slipping from where he had been caught on the arm rest. He had drooped into the water only ten minutes before. They had rushed his son to the emergency room in the first ambulance and sent a second one for him. His first memory afterward, when he finally snapped back into reality, he was talking to a police officer. She had asked him about the green bottle they had found in the car, that had been tucked under the seat. He had denied drinking that night. Twelve hours had passed since the accident. The officer never did a breathalyzer test. Had she, she would have found remnants of the bottle left in his system, enough to prove that there had been a lot in his system prior to the crash. He would have gone to jail he thought. Instead the officer let him leave the room, to go see his son in intensive care, finding him in the place he had last saw him so many times before in his dreams, where he had last saw him yesterday before he had gone back to being just a memory again. He was dead minutes later. He admitted to his wife after months of anger and accusations. She was gone a few months after that. He felt a pull, a jerking sensation dragging him back. *If crazy people don't know they're crazy, what does that make me?* He was back in the alley, still running towards home, never having left, never having been in the car he had crashed drunk so many years before. He slowed to a trot now, then stopped entirely a few feet from the steps, wondering what he was doing in the alley. He turned and looked back at the brick building. It was intact. No smoke. No fire. No corpse with its intestines slopped into the gutter. No sign of what he had just experienced. He remembered the thing. It had been a monster, no, a demon, he thought. He looked at his hand. No fresh wound. A red mark though. He slowly walked into his home, slamming the door behind him. Not caring about what might be waiting for him. He was numb. He lit a cigarette and sat on his couch. The gun's cocking mechanism jabbed him in the lower back; awkwardly he adjusted but did not remove it. He looked out the intact window and began to breath heavily. A flash came through to meet him, more lightning he thought. *I am hallucinating.* He began to try to reason to himself. *I am hallucinating. What did I look like? Did I just run down the street, yelling things about demons?* He felt the pain in his hand, saw the real mark. Lightning flashed outside again. That was real. No rain. Had he drove? He went to the kitchen and grabbed the bottle off of the counter, taking a long pull from it and went to return to the living room when he saw the box on the floor. His stomach churned. The golden liquid from the green bottle disagreeing with him. His mouth watered but he stifled it. He took it and placed it on the table. He put the butt out on the table and lit another cigarette. He reached into his pocket and tried to pull out the rolled card, thinking about what the priest had told him. The Pastor who he was now sure was never there, a dream that you remember small clips from. He produced only lint and bits. *I need a doctor.* He pointed the gun towards the door and then towards his bedroom door. He clicked the safety on.

He thought about examining his foot again. It hadn't bothered him for a day but now that some of the panic and confusion had left it hurt again. He didn't want to see how bad it was. Instead, he limped to the bathroom. He had black streaks on his face from the ash but his wounds hadn't changed. Maybe his foot hadn't either. The towel was still in the sink, still damp. He turned the water on and filled the glasses again, turning it off before it soaked the towel again in boiling water. He rubbed his face with it, scrubbing himself red, before taking his shirt off. He looked emaciated, skeletal. Each rib, both collar bones a little monument to his week long struggle. *Nope. Longer.* To his anxiety and fear and torment. It was Thursday morning, he thought. Maybe afternoon. He rubbed his armpits and chest with the towel before wrapping it around his neck and slowly working it down his back with both hands. He'd go to the doctor he thought. He wondered. Would she be there this time? He moved his face into the shattered part of the mirror and stared at himself. He put his shirt back on. As he went to leave, he saw it. An intact cell phone, on the floor, near the door. He didn't pick it up.

He had blamed her, he thought. Their father. His parents had gone to the lake with friends as they often did, only this was only the second time they had been allowed to stay home alone. She was a year older than him, she was in charge. She had been much more sheltered than him, daddy's little girl, and she was just now finding out about sex and drugs and being cool. She had decided to have a party that Friday. Enough time to clean up before Sunday. Enough time for pot and paralyzers and shots to leave her system she had told him. You're such a loser he had told her. She had wanted a small party but it quickly rose to around twenty kids. Teenagers. Thirty maybe. Fifty would be closer, and their dad's dog, Rooster, who was locked in their parents' room for the night. Inside dog, basically blind. She and some of her close friends had been drinking while he was out. When he had returned, with his friend, his sister was drunk, laughing, playing drinking games with cards around the kitchen table. Some game involving a pyramid of cards he didn't know about yet. The ceramic bear was on the table as well while a very drunk redhead was pouring shots of vodka into its broken off, hollow head. It was fairly tame he now thought, though he could smell the weed and cigarettes that were being smoked throughout the house. He had seen his opportunity quickly upon arrival. Without his sister seeing him, he had snatched a half bottle of something off of the bookcase near the entrance to the kitchen, and some beers that had been left on the floor, and went to his parents room with his friend to watch TV. He had had a beer before but never hard liquor. He was careful to keep Rooster in the room when they entered. But later, after the bottle had disappeared, he had felt sick. With reasoning only known to him at the time, he had decided he needed to go outside to vomit rather than do it in his parents on suite bathroom. Logic of a 15-year-old. He had run out the door while his friend laughed at him, throwing up a bit on the hallway wall as he ran, then again on the bushes out front that lined one side of the driveway. Rooster had followed. He had saw the dog wag slowly down the street but didn't stop him. He returned to his room and became sick once more on the floor before spinning his way through skateboard posters and hockey logos and centerfolds and eventually to sleep. He had awoken to yelling. He didn't get out of bed immediately, only later when it dawned on him that it was his parents yelling. Home early. Power outage. He had vomit on his shirt he had worn yesterday. He quietly changed into pajama pants and a different t-shirt, careful to cover the small puddle on his carpet with his clothes, clean side up, and left to question what was going on, why was there yelling. The home was fairly clean he had thought. There were no longer cans or bottles on the kitchen counter, the table, the living room, all thrown out into the neighbour's garbage bin the night before. What his sister hadn't counted on inebriated the night before was the lingering smell of the party that she thought would have time to air out. She hadn't noticed the beer cans someone had left on the far side of the couch and on the TV stand. Nor had she noticed the bit of her brother's vomit on the wall, or the two cigarette burns in the carpet which she might have been able to explain away had she been given time rather than being ambushed in her bed. Worst of all, Rooster was missing. But not for long. Later that evening, he had gotten a call from a stranger, reading their number from the silver, bone shaped tag around the neck of a white dog with reddish patches on his head and neck. He was dead, found on the side of the road by someone who didn't think it important enough to stop. He had admitted to seeing people there and while he lowered the number to an acceptable amount of people attending he had denied any involvement in the activities. She had blamed herself; someone at her party had let her out. He kept his secret.

I'm sorry. he whispered to her.

I'm sorry, he whispered to himself.

Ashes blew into his face, a heavy hot gust. He had an audience.

His eyes burned and he was blinded, coughing, sneezing out the ash. He dropped to his knees and rubbed his eyes, making it worse, then slowly better. Ash clung to the tears that tried to rinse his eyes. He stood and turned his face towards the buildings, into a window framed by brick, giving him slight respite from the wind and ash. He could see again, though blurry. The sky was deeper now, dark clouds of ash islands in a sea of dark blood being lit by flashes that lit them, brilliantly unnerving momentarily. Ashes no longer drifting down but seeming to rain harder now. He had only walked for a few blocks and forgotten where he was going, maybe nowhere, when he noticed them again. The people, staring out their dusted windows, watching him, watchers more than before. A woman in a blue dress about 40 next to a child wearing what appeared to be the same dress. A younger man suited in a set of dress blues and cap and an out of date moustache. Two little boys nearly the same age, holding hands in little bowties. A younger couple, also holding hands, in matching colours. More. All were ready. For what he didn't know. All were waiting for a show. All dressed as though they had just came from church or whatever. Better yet a funeral. He slowly turned on the sidewalk, there were more further down the street. He backed into the street now, looking up into the building he had been walking under. More people. All with same expression. Where he had seen sadness now noting. Nothing, yet hatred. As he spun back around, he felt the pistol slip down further into his waistline. *Fuck.* He had forgotten he had it on him. Get home, put it away. Whatever was going on he couldn't be here. He began to run towards the alley as the gun nearly bounced out of his jeans. He caught it, running with his finger on the trigger, scared to have it on the street but taking comfort in its security. As he got to the alley, he turned back towards the street, still walking, his jeans catching under his heels, trying to stumble him. Still watching. He thought he recognized the woman who he had seen have her neck torn through the hazy glass. He kept the gun ready.

You can get out, you know.

He slowly dragged the gun through the ashy air and pointed. It was the homeless man who had been there for almost a week. He lowered it slightly. *There was a dog*, he thought. He kept backing up towards his door.

What? He breathed the words, forced them out rather than speaking them. As he spoke, he again recognized the man. Wearing the same shoes…the flannel! He had the same one in his closet. More. His eyes, Just now noticing a cut on his cheek hidden by weeks of beard. The old man shrugged.

Kay. He paused. Do I know you?

The man stared at him over his greying beard and weather leathered skin.

It can get better. I've seen you. I knew you once.

He kept walking backwards, away, at the still open door to the garage, but slower. Silent.

It'll be better.

He stared at the man. It came. How he knew. How his voice, his face, his shoes were familiar. He was staring at himself, though weathered and destroyed in this life it was himself. He tried to speak. He stopped. He felt a pressure in his chest. No. Not now. He tried to fight but it pulled him. The light above the garage glowing brighter. He decided. Fuck you. I choose. It smiled.

He walked to the doorway. They watched, the others, the mourning, watched. Him. On the couch. Gathering supplies and walking, stumbling to the garage. Looking up, he could see himself study the screw that held the eaves to the side of the garage. He watched as he went to the truck and placed the bottle and glass inside. Two pieces. Putting weight on the top one, the screws came out easily due to time and weight. Drag them to the garage. One on the tailpipe. Open the window, get in, close the eaves in the window. He watched himself purposefully push green pills out of a silver sleeve and place them on the ash free dash. A glass filled with yellow liquid. Green bottle nearby on the floor of the white truck. He watched himself push the pills into his other hand that hung like a spoon slightly below the edge of the dash, then ladle them into the glass. He watched himself. He realized what dream, what nightmare, it wanted him to see. He swallowed the sour contents of the glass then picked the bottle up from the floor. Drank. Give it time. The thing relished. He could feel him laugh as he watched the nodding, the attempt to sleep.

No.

He closed his eyes. Tried to drown it with silence. He watched himself. Pushing on the door inside the truck, fumbling, losing strength, then gaining it.

Fuck you.

He fell out of the truck, the door giving way, landing on a piece of mud that had come loose from the truck earlier and had become hard, cutting his cheek. He crawled into the light, around the tire. He watched himself push fingers into his mouth.

Try again!

Third attempt. A green pool. Again. More. Then nothing.

It laughed at him. Not enough.

He watched himself stand, stumble, grope the concrete, stand again, leave the door open.

He followed. He was welcomed. He watched as he pushed his head against the carpet, trying to stand, instead crawling, against the wall, unable to navigate his way to the kitchen without its aid. Shuffling against the corner until he broke free to the kitchen. He didn't have words. It kept smiling, laughing, ready to pull him under, able. He watched himself lose his steadiness on the small piece of carpet in the kitchen, pull on it, trying to drag himself up, before he curled into the brown carpet and go still.

You can't have him, he said. It waited, knowing it wasn't over. He stared into the darkness. Then a knock. Mom, knocking on the open door, always kind. She poked her head in, then entered.

Hello?

I can't talk now, Mom.

He watched as she slowly entered the home. Careful to not disturb the ash on the carpet too much, upset at the condition of the place, a mother's love. She walked towards the kitchen. *Stop* he pleaded. He followed her gaze. It was him. Himself, a beggar, a preacher, all him. She cried out, tried to wake him, trying to pick him up as she last had when he was eleven, then stand. His face, pale, fresh blood no longer flowing but pooling into red swamps inside him, blue eyes slightly open, clutching a brown carpet. Not violent yet not peaceful. His mother's screams turned to thunder, as the room became dark, red, breathing again as it prepared, ready to take him. He didn't take his eyes off his mother's as she turned out of the room, and out the front door to call his father. He sunk. He knew. He could feel her sorrow, her loss. Gripping the gun tightly he looked towards his doorway from the alley. It stood there, daring him. Begging him. The darkness, the abyss of hatred that was the devil himself. The flashes of lighting grew more frequent, the ashes, the dust grew heavier, a hurricane. A storm. He walked to the door. Looking. Black. He stood, turning towards the alley now. Watching the storm. He didn't cry. Just watched. It grew angry. It spoke inside him, tried to destroy him, make him destroy himself. He didn't. It grew angrier. The winds whipped at his face. Ash and dirt stung his eyes sour in his mouth, the winds growing until he thought it might drag him away into the darkness, sanding his knuckles and scorching him, filling his lungs with fire and needles. A voice rose inside him. Not it's or his own. Something else. Saying nothing, yet knowing what it wanted him to know, hearing what it wanted him to hear. In a moment he knew.

He stood. It howled. Clawed at him, trying to clutch. Trying to drag him down, down into helplessness. Frantic. He watched. Emotionless.

I am the storm, he said to himself.

He awoke, opening his eyes. He stared at the ceiling above his bed. He had never noticed the unique patterns each tile contained. Now, he tried to draw patterns in the lines and dashes, connecting the dots in their constellations. The sun glazed his face with warmth and calm. Slowly, he folded back the blanket from his partially clothed body, standing from the bed before reorganizing the quilt to a flat position. He smiled at it. He walked slowly through the living room. The door was closed. He made his way to the kitchen, grabbing the green bottle off of the counter and placing it in the freezer where it accompanied another half bottle resting in the plastic sleeve of the door. He would do the dishes today he thought. He took a fresh glass out of the cupboard and filled it with warm water twice over drinking slowly each time. In the bathroom, he examined his face, staring at it. It was tired, dark bags under each eye, but free of blemishes and wounds save for a red scratch just above his beard on his left cheek and a scar just below his hairline. He ran his finger over it, feeling the depression it left. He turned the nob, placing his hands under the tap and collecting water before splashing it on his face, clearing away the ash and sleep. He didn't dry away the water on his face, letting it drip onto his shoulders and chest and the floor. He retrieved the box and sat on the couch, emptying its contents on the table beside his charging phone. A pistol and some bullets lay on the table. As did a bible, a small gold cross, both belonging to his grandfather many years ago, and photos. He thought about reading the book again, perhaps restarting where he gave up when he was a child. He remembered where he had stopped. He placed the chain beside the page as a bookmark and closed it. He fingered through the stack, stopping at one of two children, a ten-year-old girl and a nine-year-old boy, holding hands on a rocky beach. The both wore brightly coloured swimsuits, the girl holding her hand above her eyes to shield them from the sun and the boy missing a sandal that was never found. He turned the photo over. Pen in his mother's handwriting. Crystal, 10 & Jack, 9, Sliver Lake. He smiled at his sister. He wondered if she was dreaming. He returned the photo to the stack and thumbed through more. A Polaroid. A couple. His arms wrapped around his wife on their wedding day, both truly happy, her belly big, his tie untied and hanging lazily around his neck, her eyes winged by lines from laughter. A long time ago, it seemed. Kelly and Jack, happy once. He wondered what she was doing then, who she was with and whether she was happy. He hoped she was happy. He hoped she forgave him. A photo of a little boy sitting on his mother's lap at Christmas, clutching a stuffed pig named Sizzle, a few feet in front of a tree brightly decorated above scattered paper and little notes from Santa Claus. It was his favorite photo. The caption was his. Kelly and Jackson, first Christmas in new home. He began to cry just as he had when he took the photo, he smiled through the tears. He stared at the boy whose eyes and hair matched his, whose nose and mouth his mother's.

I'm sorry. He said.

He would be a young man now he thought. He imagined that the man he would have become would be better than he was. That they would have agreed and not fought. He sighed, wiping away the tears.

He opened the pistol and took out the bullets, careful to replace them in their box, before returning the gun to its home inside the shoe box. He placed the book and the cross wrapped within it on top. He picked up the stack of photos. His family, friends, his sister, all there underneath the photo of his son taken on his front lawn what seemed like a lifetime ago. He placed them on top of the book, taking one last look at his the boy before smiling and placing the lid on it. He knelt and pushed the box under the bed, not afraid of what might be waiting for him there, and stood back up and left the room. He looked around the place that had been his home. Ash and regret and filth. *I should clean this place,* he thought before heading towards the open door. As he walked, he didn't bother to pick up his phone from the table. He didn't think of the green bottles that occupied his freezer. Just stepped outside onto the concrete step. He didn't light a cigarette. The sky was less grey today. Less grey and less ash was falling on him. He wondered how far away the fire must be, raging out in the wilderness and causing the light ash to snow down upon him. A car drove by the gap in the alley and there was no one staring at him from the windows beyond it. A rat bobbed out from behind the dumpster to his left. It was jet black with only one red eye staring directly at him. Above him, he noticed the garage outside light was on. A faint ray of sunlight broke through the haze overhead and hit him. Something landed in his eye. Then his shoulders and hair. It was rain. Rain that he thought he had forgotten the feeling of. Covering his eyes with the canopy of his hand, he looked upwards and smiled. He could see a wedge of blue above him and in that moment, he knew. He knew that he didn't have to stay in this place. He knew that he could leave the demons that had haunted him so intensely behind. The rain mixed with the ash and mudded his hair as it began the long task of washing away the blackness of the ashes that had made this place unliveable. He walked down the steps, down the alley, towards the street, unsure of where he was going but knowing he'd find whatever it was he was looking for. The blue light, the warmth, the rain on his face felt nice.

It was a Friday.

CPSIA information can be obtained
at www.ICGtesting.com
Printed in the USA
LVHW032223031019
633101LV00013B/759